MOONLIGHT KIN
NIC

JORDAN SUMMERS

Moonlight Kin: NIC

Copyright © 2014 Jordan Summers

Formatted by IRONHORSE Formatting

ISBN-13: 978-0990445418

Werewolf Nic La Croix has been nursing a bruised heart ever since he fell for his Alpha's mate. The last thing he wants is to play white knight for a human female who has no business being in a shifter bar.

Mindy MacDougal has spent most of her life being her big sister's keeper. Just once she'd like to do something for herself. When a night on the town takes a deadly turn, an unlikely hero comes to her rescue. One kiss is all it takes to draw her into Nic's dark world. What will Mindy do when she finds out that the monster isn't under her bed, he's in it?

Prologue

A shadow of ash spread across the highway, staining the asphalt a deeper shade of gray. Fissure cracks appeared, threading their boney fingers wide until the earth bucked beneath Jerry Seaver's semi-truck. He clenched the wheel and fought to keep the heavy load from jackknifing on the road.

"Damn earthquakes," he muttered under his breath, but his heart continued to pound.

Thunder cracked in a cloudless blue sky. Jerry poked his head out the window. He squinted against the sunlight and looked around, but the only thing he could see was a green ocean of trees rocking gently in the breeze.

The fine hairs on his arms rose, along with the pressurization in the cab of his truck. Jerry's ears popped. His unease increased despite the natural beauty around him.

He wiped his hand across his grit-covered face and it came away moist. The highway stretched out in front of him with no cars in sight. There wasn't a town around for miles. Jerry was alone. The sudden change in the air reminded him just how isolated he was on this back road. Suddenly the shortcut he'd taken wasn't such a good idea.

He shifted gears and pressed his foot down. Smoke billowed out the semi's exhaust pipes as the engine strained to pick up speed. Jerry didn't want to be out here surrounded by oppressive woods any longer than necessary.

A half a mile in front of him the air shimmered like waves on a pond. It was too cool for the mirage to be heat rising from the asphalt. Jerry's foot eased off the accelerator and the truck slowed, but he wasn't about to stop. The glistening increased and the air yawned, opening wide to reveal its gaping black mouth.

"What the hell?" Jerry leaned forward to get a better look at...at...he had no idea what he was seeing. The sun gleamed off his red hood, but didn't penetrate the dark entrance ahead.

It wasn't real. It couldn't be.

"You're just tired," he muttered aloud.

Jerry rubbed his eyes and shook his head. He'd been driving for ten hours and hadn't gotten much sleep the previous night. He was determined to get to Vancouver today.

The crisp air worked to keep him awake, but wouldn't prevent hallucinations. This had to be one, because what he was witnessing didn't make sense.

He reached for his Red Bull and took the last sip. Moisture dribbled down his chin onto his shaggy beard. Jerry wiped his mouth with the back of his hand, then crushed the can and tossed it over his shoulder before grabbing another out of his cooler.

Jerry pressed the cold can to his forehead, then popped it open. He took a deep swallow, then checked to see if the *hallucination* still hovered above the road.

The tear had widened, revealing more of the gloom. If it got any bigger, it would swallow his truck. Something moved in the shadows. Fear plunged its icy fingers into him, locking on to his spine.

The gap expanded and someone—no, *something*—fell

out, then the opening snapped shut.

Jerry was too close to stop and too scared to react. His truck barreled down upon the...he squinted...*creature*, striking the black mass. A loud bang filled the cab as the shadowy thing smacked the grille and flew through the air, landing on the side of the road.

He glanced into his side mirror to see where it had gone. The black creature rose, took a few steps, then collapsed in the lane.

Jerry crossed himself and prayed that it was dead. Whatever he'd struck wasn't human, wasn't of this world. He had seen where it had come from with his own eyes and he wasn't about to stick around to find out if it was okay. With his heart in his throat, Jerry shifted gears and tore down the road.

An hour later, he pulled his rig into the truck stop and washed the blood off the grill. By the time Jerry Seaver reached Vancouver, he had convinced himself that he'd imagined the whole incident.

CHAPTER ONE

Mindy MacDougal stopped her car next to the curb. Celina Gibson opened the passenger door and handed her the pepperoni pizza, then climbed in.

The aroma of tomato sauce, oregano, and sausage filled the small cab, making Mindy's stomach growl.

"I don't know if I can wait until we get to the house to have a slice," Mindy said.

Celina buckled her seatbelt, then reached for the warm box. "If I can wait, you can wait." She glanced at Mindy. "Isn't that Izzy's shirt?"

Mindy grinned. "Yep!"

"Can't believe she let you wear it. I tried to borrow it one time and she threatened to break my fingers."

"Yeah, Izzy is weird about sharing things. She never wants anyone to wear her clothes or use her stuff. Said it made them smell funny." Mindy laughed and put her blinker on, then pulled away from the curb. "If she didn't want me to wear her clothes then she shouldn't have left them in the closet when she moved out."

"I still can't believe she's gone," Celina said.

Mindy squeezed her hand. "I know you miss her, too."

Celina and Isabel had been best friends for a few years, then this last year Izzy pulled away. It was a pattern she repeated when anyone got too close. To soothe Celina's hurt feelings, Mindy had stepped in as a surrogate for her sister. She wasn't as good company as Izzy, but she did her best.

"She was always threatening to move. I just didn't think she'd go through with it. I mean, where else is she going to get such a sweet setup?" Celina asked.

"What do you mean?" Mindy glanced at her.

"You paid her rent. You did her laundry. You bought all the food. Isabel never had to do anything while you were around." Bitterness tinged her tone.

Mindy's face heated. "It was my choice. She never asked me to do any of those things."

"She never had to," Celina retorted. "Wish I had a younger sister like you."

Mindy sighed. How could she explain in a way that Celina would understand?

She hadn't always been the responsible one. There was a time when she and Izzy had been footloose and carefree. That was before Izzy's penchant for outlandish storytelling took a dark turn, before the expensive psychiatrists, before the psych meds, before all the experimental treatments.

Nothing their parents tried could eliminate Izzy's "visions" or quell her talk of monsters. To this day, her sister was utterly convinced of their existence.

The treatments did succeed in one area. They successfully changed Mindy and Izzy's relationship. Her role in the family dynamic evolved from close ally to her sister's keeper.

The change hadn't been easy for Mindy. At first, she'd chafed at carrying so much responsibility. She missed her freedom. She missed having fun. But there was only room for one bad girl at the table and Izzy had claimed the spot.

Now that Izzy was gone and Mindy was finally free, she didn't know quite what to do with herself.

Celina chewed on her bottom lip. "Did she at least say goodbye before she left?"

She did her best to hide her pain, but Mindy didn't think she was successful. "You know my sister. Goodbyes are so...responsible. She called you, though, didn't she?"

"Yeah, but she didn't tell me that she'd moved out," Celina said.

"Then what did she say?" Mindy asked.

"She told me to watch out for the monsters," she said.

Mindy rolled her eyes. "What's that supposed to mean?"

Celina shrugged and looked away, but not before Mindy saw fear in her eyes.

"Don't let her freak you out," she said.

"You know, this might turn out to be a good thing in disguise," Celina said. "You've been taking care of your sister for years. Izzy could do with a serious dose of reality."

Mindy knew she was right, but it would take some time to adjust to all the changes.

"She's your big sister. It's past time that she acts like it," Celina said.

"We're only a year apart," Mindy said. "Not exactly a huge gap."

"Doesn't matter. She's still older," Celina said. "Have you heard from her since she left?"

"She called Wednesday night, but I was at school," Mindy said.

"Did she at least leave a message?"

Mindy hesitated. "Yeah, sort of."

"Uh-oh. What did she say?" Celina asked.

Mindy sighed. "Maybe you can make sense of her message. She said the winds told her it was time to move on. That there was darkness coming."

Celina's perfectly shaped brow shot up. "The winds? Darkness? Last time I checked, wind didn't talk. And darkness"—she looked out the window—"comes every night. Did she tell you anything useful? Like where she was going?"

The question surprised Mindy. She thought for sure Izzy would've told her best friend where she was going. But one look at Celina's face made it clear that she hadn't. Weird. Should she tell her? She couldn't see any harm in letting her know.

"Apparently, the winds gave my sister directions to New Orleans." She laughed.

Celina gasped.

"What is it?" Mindy asked.

"Nothing," Celina said.

"Tell me."

"I just always wanted to go there. Izzy and I talked about it a lot. She said we'd run away there one day." Celina grew quiet. "Guess that won't be happening now. She'll fit right in down there."

That was what worried Mindy. What if Izzy didn't come back? What if there was no room in her 'new' life for her sister?

"I hope she's okay," Mindy said.

"You need to stop worrying about her," Celina said. There was sternness in her voice that hadn't been there a moment ago.

She was right, but the saying about old habits dying hard was true. "It's what sisters do," Mindy said quietly. She was surprised Celina wasn't more concerned given how much she knew about Izzy, but maybe she was in shock about New Orleans.

"I know you love her, but your sister is a flake. You have to live your own life now," Celina said. "It's past time Izzy learns to stand on her own two feet."

Mindy didn't want to think about Izzy anymore. It would mean examining her own sorry life. "So what's on the agenda tonight?" she asked.

"I thought we'd go for a Ryan double feature." Celina reached into her purse and pulled out two DVDs. "Dibs on

Gosling."

"Man," Mindy said. "That's not fair."

Celina laughed. "Like settling for Reynolds is such a hardship."

Mindy glanced at her and smiled. "True. I wouldn't exactly kick him out of my bed."

"No woman with a brain in her head would."

Lights faded away as they drove out of town and made a right onto a back road that would eventually lead to Mindy's home.

Thick woods on both sides of the road swallowed what little light came from the headlights. Mindy cranked the radio and pressed on the accelerator. The miles rolled by.

Celina was doing her best pop princess impersonation when Mindy spotted the entrance to a long drive.

"Hey." She nudged Celina. "Is that the road you take to get to that club you're always talking about? Pits or something."

Celina stopped singing and looked out the window. "Yeah, that's it," she said reluctantly. "The place is called Sticks." She crossed her arms over her chest and sank down in her seat. "Izzy never really liked it. She said the place made her feel uncomfortable. She only went there a few times."

"Really?" Mindy asked. "I was always under the impression that Izzy liked it. Well, as much as she liked anyplace."

"No!" Celina said. "The only time she ever wanted to go there was when she had the urge to dance."

Dancing was one of the few passions she and her sister shared these days, but they rarely indulged in the activity at the same time.

"Can't believe that I've driven by the entrance so many times and never noticed it before," Mindy said. "For some reason, I could've sworn that you and Izzy told me it was on the east side." She was positive they had.

Celina laughed off her comment, then shifted in her seat. "You aren't exactly Ms. Observant," she remarked.

It was common knowledge around the animal clinic that Mindy was driven and focused, but only on work and school. What little time remained had gone toward caring for Izzy and protecting her.

Mindy stared at the entrance through her side mirror until it faded into the night. "Now that I know where it is I'll have to go," she said.

Celina cleared her throat and picked at the edge of the pizza box. "I'm not sure Sticks is your kind of place." She stared out the window as she spoke.

Mindy frowned. "What do you mean? You said it was fun. You told me there were tons of good-looking men. I know you've been going there just about every weekend with your friend Erin. Izzy went with you last week." She took a breath. "In fact, you've gone there with everyone but me."

"Isabel didn't have a good time," Celina said softly. "She hated it so much that she made me promise not to take you there."

Why would her sister do that? Mindy vaguely remembered Izzy coming home freaked out, but since that wasn't unusual, she hadn't been concerned at the time. Now she was.

Though she'd never shown it, Mindy's feelings had been hurt that Celina had never invited her to go with them to the bar. Had she asked, Mindy may have very well declined the invitation, but Celina had never bothered.

"Why would Izzy ask you to make that promise?"

"Why does Izzy say or do anything?" Celina asked, smoothly deflecting the question. "To find out the answer, you'd have to ask your sister."

They both knew that would never happen.

"Did anything unusual happen the last night you guys were there?" Mindy asked.

Celina readjusted the pizza box on her lap. "Not that I recall. It was a blast like always."

"Then I don't get why you and Izzy think I should avoid it," Mindy said.

"I can't speak for your crazy sister," Celina said. "But knowing you and knowing Sticks the way I do, I can honestly tell you it's not your type of place."

Why is Sticks great for Celina, but not for me?

Appearance-wise, they were polar opposites. Celina was tall, had long, dark hair, sun-kissed skin, a stunning face, and a trim figure that models would kill for.

Mindy had learned to live with being vertically challenged. Her curvy body was made for a different era—an era that didn't give side-eye to a woman who enjoyed eating a whole sandwich and a side of chips.

"Don't think you're going to get away with that answer without explaining yourself," Mindy said.

"You know what I mean," Celina said.

Mindy shook her head. "No, I don't. What exactly is *my* type of place?" She immediately pictured a library and rolled her eyes. How long had Celina and her sister been conspiring behind her back? It made her angry that between them they'd decided what was and wasn't good for her. How dare they after everything she'd done! She was the poster child for responsible behavior.

Celina's face pinched.

"Spill it!" Mindy wasn't about to let her off the hook.

Celina sighed. "You're more of a coffee bar kind of girl. Sticks is wild. Most nights it's a free-for-all."

Mindy's heart sank. "Are you saying I'm not any fun?" Celina wouldn't be the first one of her friends to imply she didn't know how to have a good time. Being her sister's keeper had left little time for a social life. The added responsibility had cost Mindy a lot of friendships over the years.

There were times, though—in the dead of night—that

Mindy wondered if her sacrifice had been worth it. Wondered what would've happened if, just once, she had shrugged off her responsibilities and kicked up her heels.

Celina's brown eyes widened. "I didn't say you weren't fun," she insisted.

"No, you implied it." Mindy frowned as childhood taunts of "Monotonous Mindy" echoed in her head. She wasn't monotonous. Not anymore. She could have fun. There was no one to hold her back now. Tears unexpectedly made her eyes burn. She blinked them away before Celina noticed.

"I'm sorry. I didn't mean to hurt your feelings," Celina said. "It's just that Sticks isn't your typical bar. It's really rowdy. Fights are common. Most of the guys that go there are...*different*. You're used to hipsters, not the kind of chest-beating, blue-collar he-men that frequent Sticks."

Mindy glowered. "I like he-men. I just haven't met many in real life." Try never.

She wasn't lying about being attracted to those types of guys. Or *any* type of guy, for that matter. It had been a long time since Mindy had dated. Her dry spell now resembled the Mohave. She was willing to try anything at this point.

"And I enjoy going to wild places on occasion," she said.

Celina snorted. "Name one wild place you've gone to. Seriously, just one. Before you answer, I want the dates, too, because I can't remember the last time you went to a rowdy bar," she said. "For as long as I've known you, you've planned your 'impulsive' moments."

"That's not true."

"Yes, it is," Celina said.

Heat spread up Mindy's neck and into her face. She took her eyes off the road. "Perhaps if you'd invited me to go along with you just once, we wouldn't be having this argument." Her voice cracked.

Celina patted her arm. "I told you that Izzy didn't want me to. She made me promise."

"Well, Izzy isn't here anymore. This isn't about her. This

is *my* life we're talking about, not my sister's," Mindy grumbled.

Maybe Celina and Izzy were right. Maybe she wasn't any fun. Maybe her sister had inherited all the fun genes in the family. That would explain why Celina always took her other friends to Sticks and left her at home.

Celina glanced out the windshield and slammed her hands against the dashboard. "Mindy, look out!"

Chapter Two

They were going to die! And it was all because she didn't get invited to a bar. The black mass lying halfway in her lane grew larger and larger as she bore down upon it.

Mindy screamed and jerked the wheel to the right, missing the object by inches. Her tires screeched and her heart did its best to crack her ribs. She hit the brakes and the car skidded dangerously before coming to a stop in the center of the road.

She pressed a hand to her chest and looked in her rearview mirror to make sure no one was behind them. Darkness met her.

"What was that?" Mindy asked. She hadn't gotten a good look at it. She'd been too busy trying not to hit it.

"Not sure. A bear, maybe?" Celina slowly released the dash. "That was close." She looked over her shoulder. "Turn around so your headlights illuminate it. I want to get another look at it."

With shaky hands, Mindy managed a three-point turn. The massive animal came into view. "I think you're right about it being a bear." Nothing else outside the zoo could be that large. She couldn't see the beast's face, but its crumpled body was almost as tall as the hood of her compact car.

"No, it's the wrong shape." Celina squinted. "We need to get more light on it."

Mindy hit her high beams, illuminating the road and more of the animal.

They both gasped.

Whatever it was, it was massive. Really massive. "It has to be a bear. A grizzly from the size of it. There's nothing else in the wild around here that big," Mindy said.

"Buffalos are," Celina said.

"That isn't a buffalo," Mindy said.

"I know," Celina said. "Only one way to find out for sure."

Mindy squinted at the animal through her bug-stained windshield. "Do you think it's dead? It looks dead."

"Yeah," Celina said. "I think it's dead. We need to get it off the road."

Mindy glanced at her. "Have you been lifting weights without telling me? There's no way we're going to be able to move it, unless we cut it up."

Celina scrunched her nose. "Ew! I'm not cutting anything up. If need be, we'll hook your tow chain around it and pull it off the road. If we leave it there, someone's going to hit it and total their car."

"Looks like it's already been hit." Mindy checked the deserted road to see if there was a car lying in the ditch. "I don't see any wreckage." She also didn't spot any broken glass. "Maybe someone shot it."

Celina paled. "Let's hope not," she said. "That wouldn't be good for anyone involved."

It might not be good, but it was common for the area. Mindy pulled over to the side of the road and parked. She flipped on her hazards and kept her headlights trained on the animal.

Celina unbuckled her seatbelt and climbed out of the car. Mindy walked to her trunk and popped it open, then grabbed two pairs of latex gloves. She pulled a pair on, then handed the other set to Celina.

"I don't see a lot of blood." Celina moved closer to examine the animal. "Holy crap! It's still breathing."

The news startled Mindy. She'd thought for sure the animal was dead. "Get away from it," she said. "It might attack out of fear and pain."

Celina glowered at her. "I've been working at the animal clinic longer than you have. I may not be a veterinary student, but I know what I'm doing."

Mindy sighed. "I didn't mean anything by it. I just don't want you to get hurt."

School was a sore subject for Celina. She'd had to go to work to help support her parents and had never managed to finish high school. After they died, she'd eventually gotten her GED, but the achievement had done little to ease her insecurities.

Mindy had encouraged her to continue her education, but Celina had balked. She'd claimed that if Izzy didn't need a degree, then neither did she.

As excuses went, it was pretty sad. But not nearly as sad as the real reason Celina had no interest in going back to school.

The real reason she hadn't bothered to better her life was because Celina was waiting for a knight in shining armor to come and sweep her off her feet. It was a fantasy she clung to and it was just as real to her as monsters were to Izzy. Celina wanted that knight more than anything and wouldn't settle for less.

Years of looking after Izzy had taught Mindy that you couldn't change someone, especially once they'd made up their minds.

"I'm going to move in closer to see if it has any other obvious injuries," Celina said.

"Are you sure it's alive?" Mindy couldn't see any movement. Maybe what Celina had witnessed was the body settling after death.

"I just saw its chest rise again," Celina said. "I'm pretty sure that means it's alive."

Mindy took a deep breath. She wanted to point out that she was the one with the medical training, but didn't want to upset Celina any more than she already had. "Is it a bear?"

"No," Celina said. "It's canine."

"That's not possible," Mindy said. "It's too large."

Celina tore her gaze away. "Pretty sure the animal in the road is definitive proof that you're wrong."

Mindy ignored her sarcasm. "I don't have the instruments or equipment with me to tend its wounds and I don't have pain meds to ease its suffering."

"I know," Celina said. "Help me get it into the car."

Mindy glanced at the animal and then at her compact car. "There's no way it's going to fit," she said.

"It'll fit." Celina sounded so confident.

Too bad Mindy didn't feel the same. She hesitated.

"If we can get it to the clinic, then Dr. Fields might be able to save it or at least make sure it doesn't suffer more," Celina said.

Her friend was determined to save the animal. Mindy appreciated her tenacity, but found it odd since Celina had always kept her distance from all the animals that were brought into the clinic.

Up until tonight, Mindy was the only one who'd regularly rallied to save the animal kingdom. Maybe her passion was finally rubbing off on Celina.

Mindy approached cautiously. The animal was larger up close. Celina had to be wrong about the species. A quick cursory examination proved otherwise. What kind of canine grew to this size?

"Celina, I really don't think he's going to fit."

"He'll fit. Trust me."

She didn't think so, but Celina was right—they couldn't leave the creature here for someone to hit. Who knows how long it had been suffering. Mindy couldn't bear to see any animal injured and in pain.

"I'll move the seats forward." Celina raced to the car and adjusted the seats.

Mindy stared at the animal. She'd never seen anything quite like it. Its head was wide, wider than a typical canine, and it had a mouthful of sharp teeth. Sable fur covered its broad body. She glanced at its paws. They were canine in shape, but its claws looked like something more suited for a grizzly bear.

"I'm embarrassed to admit this, but I can't identify this animal." Mindy hadn't grown up in the area, so she wasn't familiar with every species, but thanks to school she had a pretty good grasp of the natural habitats of predators. "It sort of looks like a wolf, but it's too big and its head isn't the right shape."

The biggest wolf Mindy had ever seen had weighed 175 pounds. This one was *much* larger.

"Have you ever seen anything like it?" she asked.

Celina's gaze skittered away. "You grab the back end, I'll lift its head."

Mindy watched in horror as Celina whispered something in the creature's ear. The animal shuddered.

"Seriously, be careful," Mindy said. "I know you're trying to soothe it, but an injured animal this size can do a lot of damage." She glanced at her car. "I wish I would've thought to carry a muzzle."

"I doubt it would fit, even if you had brought one," Celina said.

Mindy glanced at the creature's mouth. *No,* she thought. *Probably not.*

After thirty minutes of grunting, dragging, and shoving, they got the injured canine in the backseat of Mindy's car. Surprisingly, it fit, when everything about its body said it shouldn't have. Maybe its size was deceptive due to the thick fur? At one point, Mindy could've sworn the animal was helping them, but it was just wishful thinking on her part.

Celina's knees touched the dash and the cold pizza box was crushed to her chest, as Mindy raced to the animal clinic in Breakbend, Oregon. Fifteen minutes outside of town, she dug her phone out of her purse and tossed it to Celina.

"Call Dr. Fields and tell him we're on our way," she said.

Celina punched in the number. "You know he's going to ask you to assist," she said.

Mindy glanced at her, afraid to take her eyes off the road for long at this speed. "Of course, that's my job. It's what I'm training to do."

Breakbend's lights twinkled in the darkness, illuminating the western facades covering the businesses on the main drag.

Mindy slowed when they came into town, but they still reached the clinic in record time. Celina pried herself out of the car and tossed the pizza onto her vacated seat. She was digging for the keys to the front door when Dr. Fields showed up.

"What do we have, Mindy?" he asked.

"Canine of some kind," she said. "Looks like it's been hit by a car, but it could've been shot. I haven't located any entrance or exit wounds, but won't know for sure until it's been X-rayed. We found him lying on the side of the road. We got out to move it and discovered he was still alive."

Dr. Fields poked his head into the car to take a look. His brow slowly furrowed. "Not a lot of visible blood, but no doubt there are internal injuries. Where did you say you were when you found it?"

"Off the highway. On the back road between Breakbend and Carson, not far from Telegraph Road. We were headed to my house."

"I'm surprised it fit in the car," he said.

"You and me both," Mindy said.

Celina came out of the clinic with a gurney.

"Help me get it on the table," Dr. Fields said. "Be careful.

We don't want to do more damage."

Once again Celina and Mindy grabbed a section of the canine and lifted, then helped the doctor wheel it into the operating room.

After a quick set of X-rays ruled out a gunshot wound, Mindy pulled scrubs on over her clothes and administered the anesthetic under the vet's supervision.

"He's under," she said, monitoring its vitals, before making sure the animal received enough oxygen.

The doctor's frown deepened as he analyzed the X-rays for other injuries. "That's odd. Only one bone appears to be broken. Given its lethargic state, I expected the damage to be much worse."

"That's good, right?" Mindy asked.

"No, that means it's in shock. That can kill it just as effectively as an untreated injury. I'll have to open him up to be sure we're not missing anything vital."

Dr. Fields made the incision, then carefully repaired a couple of minor tears on one of the organs. After a thorough search to make sure he hadn't missed any other trauma, he closed the animal up and aligned the bone, then put a cast on the leg.

"Is he going to be okay?" Mindy asked.

"He should be, but I simply cannot explain his condition. With these minor injuries, the animal should've been up and moving around," he said, his expression troubled. "Albeit slowly."

"Do you know what it is?" Mindy asked.

"A mystery," he said.

"I mean, do you know what kind of animal it is?" she asked.

He pulled his bloody gloves off and tossed them into the HAZMAT container. "I'm not entirely certain," he said. "I've never seen anything quite like him, especially in the lupine family. It's almost as if someone bred a Russian wolf with a Caucasian Mountain dog, which would be hard to do without the wolf trying to kill the dog. But then again, those dogs are tough."

"I'm not familiar with that breed," Mindy said.

"It's also known as the Russian Bear dog for obvious reasons. The males can grow to be over two hundred pounds. They make perfect guard dogs."

"I can see why. I wouldn't want to take one on," Mindy said. "But this isn't Russia."

"No, but people have all kinds of exotic pets that they shouldn't own," he said. "I've pulled some of its blood for a DNA check. We'll know more once we get the results. In the meantime, let's get him into recovery. I think we have one cage big enough in the back."

"If he fit in my backseat, we can get him into the bear cage," Mindy said.

* * * * *

Celina watched through the small window in the door as Mindy and Dr. Fields wheeled the massive wolf toward the back room. She'd been eavesdropping on their conversation, so she'd heard the doctor order the DNA test.

She couldn't let them see the results when they came in. Celina had to get to them first, so she could switch them out with another canine. Since she received all the paperwork and documentation coming into the office, it should be simple enough to do.

The doctor and Mindy were baffled by the unique discovery, but Celina wasn't. She'd immediately identified the creature they'd found on the side of the road.

Sure, the animal looked a little different from the others. Less wolf, more monster, perhaps. Celina hadn't recognized it immediately, but once she'd gotten closer, she'd known.

She peered at it one last time before it disappeared into the recovery room. Its body was bigger and its head a few inches wider than the others of its kind. Its teeth looked longer and sharper, too. The only really surprising thing about the whole situation was that the animal was injured at all.

Celina had seen them in their other form many times. Watched them fight until they were bloody and almost unrecognizable. Each and every time they'd risen like nothing had happened. She'd always assumed they were invincible or close to it. The news that they weren't came as a relief.

No, there was no mistaking the massive animal lying on the table, but Celina couldn't exactly go in and tell them that they'd found a werewolf. A real, honest-to-goodness werewolf.

A thrill shot through her and Celina clasped her hands together. Today was her lucky day. She had prayed for an opportunity like this. Hoped it would occur. But deep down, never thought it would happen. Yet here it was laid out in front of her like a gift from above. It was a sign. The sign she'd been waiting for.

Izzy's warning floated in her head. *If you don't stay away from the monsters, they're going to end up killing you.*

Her best friend was wrong. Unlike Izzy, Celina wasn't afraid of these creatures. She understood them. They weren't all that different from humans. There were both good and bad ones. It was a distinction Izzy rarely made. She loved her best friend, but Celina wasn't about to pass up this chance.

It was the perfect opportunity to spend more than a single night with one of the Moonlight Kin. Be more than a chew toy that they nibbled on, rutted in, then passed around for others to sample.

Contrary to what those *Weres* believed, Celina wasn't anyone's plaything.

She tugged her shirt down to cover the scratches she'd received last week from her *date*. Marco had been a particularly energetic lover, but like the others, he hadn't bothered to call her after she'd gotten him off.

Celina had really thought that he liked her, until she saw him around town with another woman. Their eyes met, but Marco hadn't acknowledged her. She'd thought about confronting him, but Weres never responded well to aggression. Celina wouldn't have to worry about Marco after tonight.

A plan formulated in her head as she waited for Mindy to finish up. She'd nurse this one back to health and imprint her scent on it. All Celina needed to do was prove to the Were that she could care for it, make the creature feel indebted to her, then she would get him to claim her as his mate.

* * * * *

Mindy helped Dr. Fields get the animal into the cage. She stroked its head and cooed softly to it, to reassure the canine that it was safe.

"It won't wake up for a while," Dr. Fields said.

"I know," she said. "I just like to believe that it can hear me and knows that we're taking care of it."

He gave her a tired smile. "You have a good heart, Mindy, but I do worry about this job being too hard on you."

"I'm tougher than I look," Mindy said. A tongue brushed against the back of her hand. "He licked me."

Dr. Fields looked in the cage. "He couldn't have. He's still asleep and will be for a few more hours. You probably just brushed against his mouth."

Mindy frowned and looked at the snoring canine. She knew the difference between a lick and a brush. It had definitely been a lick. But since that type of thing wasn't worth arguing over, she let it go.

"I'm going to head home now."

Dr. Fields yawned. "Me too. See you in the afternoon."

Mindy glanced at her watch and winced. She was going to be a zombie in class tomorrow if she didn't get some sleep. The Ryans would have to wait for another girls' night. She looked at the animal and gave him one last pet, then turned off the lights.

"Goodnight, puppy," she murmured and left the room.

* * * * *

Mindy didn't see the black wolf raise its head. She didn't see its eyes begin to glow. She didn't see it lick its lips so it could taste her skin again. And she didn't hear it sniff the air, locking in her scent, so it would be able to find her again.

CHAPTER THREE

Gravel crunched under Nic La Croix's truck tires as he turned onto the long driveway. Trees and dense underbrush lined the road, leading him deeper into the woods. He ran his hand through his shaggy hair and the tension in his muscles released as wilderness surrounded him.

Nic didn't have long to enjoy the feeling. The tightness came right back as a steady thump, thump, thump reached his ears. So much for convening with nature. After a quarter-mile, the trees parted to reveal a crude gravel parking lot.

On the far side of the lot, a large wooden structure squatted like a toad against the tree-line. The roof slanted to the left and looked to be under imminent threat of collapse. Chipped red paint covered the front of the building, while ignoring the sides. The splash of color did little to disguise the building's deteriorated condition.

A flashing pink neon sign hung above the entrance to the bar. The first "T" and the last "S" of its name were burned out. Instead of spelling "Sticks", the sign now read "Sick."

The new name is more fitting for the shifter bar, Nic thought.

He stared at the crowded lot, debating whether to leave.

The only parking spots left bordered the trees and were nowhere near the entrance. Not that it was a problem. The position would make it easier to get out when the time came. Nic looked at his watch. Not yet six o'clock and already packed. It would only get worse.

After a hard day's work, he wanted a beer, but Nic wasn't sure fighting the crowd would be worth it this close to the full moon. He glanced up at the sky. The sun hadn't set yet and the moon was already rising. Its pregnant appearance made all wolves anxious, but was especially difficult for the younger ones, who thought they had something to prove.

Restlessness snaked its way through Nic's body, leaving him edgy. The feeling was happening more and more lately, but had nothing to do with the moon and everything to do with not being bondmated.

Nic listened to the steady beat of the music and heard a crowd roar. The sound quickly morphed into howls. Blood simmered in his veins as he fought the urge to join in.

It had been two months since he'd moved off Aidan Fortier's estate and away from the pack. Two months since he'd sworn off fickle human females.

He'd always fallen too hard and too fast for his own good. It had gotten him hurt on more than one occasion, but this time had been the worst because he'd fallen for his Alpha's mate.

Nic couldn't bear to be around Aidan's mate, Jenna Dane, feeling the way he felt about her. Every day he watched her belly ripen with Aidan's child, and he couldn't help thinking what if...

It didn't matter that it was the man in him that wanted her, not the wolf. Pain was pain.

Next month Jenna would give birth, thanks to shifters' short gestation periods. Pregnancy wouldn't be possible if she wasn't truly Aidan's bondmate, but seeing her expectant, glowing, and happy only compounded his loneliness.

Maybe someday he'd get used to sleeping alone, but Nic

had his doubts.

Once a pack animal, always a pack animal.

Being homesick for his pack was why he found himself at Sticks and not home at the little house he'd rented outside of town. The desire for a beer and to be around his own kind was a temptation he couldn't resist. Nic drove to the tree line and threw the truck into park, then climbed out. One beer, then he'd leave. Okay, maybe one and a half. It would take a lot more than that to impair a Were.

The music pumped hard, vibrating his chest as he strode toward the bar. There wasn't a cover charge for shifters, only humans. Not that many humans came out to this place or even knew about it. And the ones that did, knew the score going in.

Weres had groupies, just like rock bands. Their animalistic, insatiable nature drew them from hundreds of miles away. The humans who partied at Sticks came here for one reason and one reason only—to hook up with a shifter.

Nic wasn't looking for company, and he certainly wasn't looking for a fight, but he did want a beer. A nice cold one. For that, he'd put up with the loud music and the boisterous crowd.

"Hey, Derek," Nic said. "How's it going?"

The burly doorman grinned, flashing long canines. "Different day, same shit."

"I hear you. Lucien Bellard working tonight?" Nic asked.

His best friend bartended most nights, but he did get off work on occasion. When that happened, he didn't show up here. He took off for the mountains.

"Yep, he's behind the bar, keeping a close eye on the pups," Derek said. "A bunch of them came in earlier itching to test their claws. Remember when you were that young?"

Nic laughed. "Hell no! I was never that young."

Derek chuckled. "Me neither."

It was common for young Weres to come to Sticks. The place allowed them to blow off steam and test their skills.

Pack life was all about hierarchy. Young wolves were constantly looking for ways to better their positions. Nic didn't have to worry about that anymore. He'd earned his spot in Aidan's west coast pack through blood, brains, and brute strength.

Nic leaned forward and waited for Derek to sniff him. It didn't matter who or what you were, everyone got sniffed on their way into Sticks. It was a surefire way to keep out the troublemakers and to identify the humans. If you weren't pack, you got your hand stamped with a wolf paw. It was an inside joke that only regulars recognized.

"You're good to go." Derek hiked his thumb over his shoulder. "You came on the right night. The band's supposed to be good tonight."

"Probably won't stay that long," Nic said. "Just here for a beer."

The bouncer shrugged, then gave him a look that said "suit yourself."

The inside of the bar was even more crowded than the parking lot. Most of the worn tables were already occupied, and the only stool available sat at the end of the long, polished oak bar. Weres lined the bar three deep. They kicked up sawdust beneath their feet as they waited to get served.

Nic made his way to the end of the bar and scanned the crowd. He didn't think many from Aidan's compound would be there, but it didn't hurt to check. He wouldn't mind shooting the breeze with a familiar face.

A dark head popped up above the crowd. Lucien waved to him, his green eyes glittering mischievously.

Nic nodded in acknowledgment. It had been a while since he and Lucien had had a chance to catch up, but it didn't look like that would change tonight.

Two pups knocked younger Weres aside as they pushed their way to the front of the crowd. Nic didn't recognize them, which didn't mean much since the west coast

Moonlight Kin were spread out over several states, but he did recognize the type.

Impatience oozed from their pores. Some pups naturally fell into their pack position. Others fought for purchase. These two fell into the latter camp. Their stance screamed aggression. In a shifter bar, that was a good way to get your ass kicked.

Nic watched dispassionately as they stopped at the bar and waved money in front of Lucien's face. *I wouldn't do that if I were you,* he thought. His best friend didn't have a lot of patience for assholes.

Lucien's lip curled and a growl rumbled out of his wide chest. The Celtic tattoos that started at his neck and encased both arms rippled as he tensed. Smart pups took a step back to give Lucien space. The two with the money in their hands didn't move.

Some pups just had to learn the hard way.

A claw came out and speared the money, yanking the bills from the closest pup's hand. Lucien tossed the money into a tip jar, then yelled, "Next!"

The startled pup opened his mouth to complain, but must've got a look at Lucien's expression and changed his mind.

Nic sighed. He wasn't in the mood to put up with this kind of crap tonight. He turned to leave, but before he could go, a beer slid down the bar and stopped in front of him.

He looked over in time to see Lucien grin, then his friend went back to filling orders. The two pups who'd been flashing money glared at him. Nic raised his pint glass in salute, then took a deep swig. The cold, crisp flavor of hops and barley exploded on his tongue. He leaned his back against the edge of the bar and scanned the crowd.

Several groupies had already snagged a table near the front, close to the band. The location put them in the position to be seen by everyone, which Nic supposed was the point.

The band was still setting up their equipment. He

couldn't tell if they were human or not. He spotted a few wolf paw stamps in the crowd, but not many. Nic made a mental note to avoid them and went back to enjoying his beer.

A few minutes later there was a knock on the bar. Nic turned to find Lucien smiling at him.

"You look miserable as ever," Nic said.

His friend had a perpetual smile on his face and took delight in the little things, especially if those things came in the form of aggravating a friend. But there was more to Lucien than that. Every once in a while the mask would slip and Nic would glimpse the darkness he kept hidden from the world.

Nic had never asked what caused the shadows. He figured if Lucien wanted to let him know, he would. Until then, he'd be there whenever his friend needed him and would continue to keep up pretenses.

"You're the one lurking at the end of the bar, my friend. How do you expect to meet anyone with that sour expression on your face?" Lucien asked.

"I don't," Nic said. "I'm just here for the beer and your stellar company."

Lucien laughed. "Then you're in luck, because tonight I am in rare form."

"I can see that." Nic indicated to the pups jockeying for position.

Lucien followed his gaze, and his green eyes glittered with deadly intent. "The problems they present can be easily solved with a quick trip around back."

"Is that what you plan to do later?" Nic asked, eyeing his friend.

"Ah, *mon ami*, I'm a lover, not a fighter. You know that." Lucien winked.

Nic snorted. Lucien was definitely a lover. He *loved* women. Nic had seen him with an endless string of ladies. One look from the dark-haired, green-eyed Frenchman and women fell to their knees. None of them stayed long, and that suited Lucien just fine. In that respect, they were polar opposites. Nic wanted nothing more than to have a mate to go home to at the end of the day.

As for not being a fighter, there was no way in hell his friend could ever convince him that was the case. The darkness in his green gaze was no illusion. He hadn't come by it from anything other than pain.

"What do you have to do to get a drink around here?" someone shouted.

The muscles in Lucien's arms flexed and his hands tightened on the bar. Lucien's nails lengthened, burrowing into the grainy fibers. Nic heard the wood groan under the pressure.

"You'd better get going, Lover Boy, before the crowd turns on you," Nic said.

Lucien glanced at him. "It wouldn't be the first time." His smile returned, but with a touch of melancholy. *"Au revoir, mon ami."*

* * * * *

Mindy stared at the lights in the distance and debated whether to turn her car around. Coming here had seemed like a good idea.

She'd told Celina that she knew how to have fun. It still irked her that Izzy had made Celina promise never to bring her here. Despite her irritation with the women, it had still taken Mindy two weeks to work up the courage to come.

Not that it mattered anymore. Izzy was gone and Celina no longer cared what Mindy did. She was too preoccupied with her new boyfriend, Slade. They'd been dating for a little over a week, which was positively long term for Celina. Every time Mindy saw them together, which wasn't often, they appeared to be joined at the tongue.

She was genuinely happy that Celina had finally found a

steady guy, who liked her for who she was, but it also drove home the fact that Mindy went home to an empty house every night.

Mindy stared out the window. The only parking spaces left were by the woods far away from the entrance. Not the safest of locations. She should just go. This was insane.

No one in their right mind went to a bar alone, especially a woman. Wasn't she always telling Celina that? Yet here she sat outside of Sticks, considering whether to go inside.

Mindy tried to remember the last time she'd hit the bars. Between college classes and work, there hadn't been a lot of time to socialize.

If her calculations were correct—and they were—then it had been a year since she'd painted the town red. Okay, mauve. With her sister gone, she couldn't use Izzy as an excuse for not having a social life anymore. The music thumped and her body automatically swayed in her seat.

Just one dance, a little voice in her head whispered. *One dance won't hurt anyone.*

Neither Celina nor Izzy would ever know that she'd been there. Especially if she didn't stay long.

The music called out to her with its siren song. Mindy wanted to be the fun person she used to be before everything changed. She wanted to experience that kind of freedom again, if only for one night. Was that so much to ask?

She parked her car and climbed out. Gravel crunched under her shoes. Mindy glanced at her vintage pumps. They weren't made for traversing rock, but she saw no other way to get to the bar, unless she suddenly sprouted wings. Mindy apologized to her favorite pair of shoes, then toddled to the entrance.

Her footsteps faltered when she caught sight of the man checking IDs at the door. Barrel chested with arms the size of telephone poles, the man wore faded blue jeans and a ripped T-shirt that had some kind of biker emblem on it that she didn't recognize.

When his gaze landed on her, his light green eyes appeared to glow in the dark. The illusion only lasted a moment, but it was long enough for Mindy. Stories of monsters flooded her mind. She wanted to turn tail and run, but she wasn't dressed for sprinting. Mindy's knees locked in place.

How many years had she put her own wishes aside to cater to her sister's whims? How many lies had she told on her behalf? Mindy couldn't allow Izzy's dark fantasies to prevent her from living her life. Not anymore.

Instead of running, she forced herself to focus on her clothes. Mindy tugged at the skirt of her vintage red dress, though it already dropped below her knees. The nice outfit usually made her feel pretty and confident. But right now she'd willingly trade the dress and her favorite shoes for a comfy pair of jeans.

The doorman came out of the shadowed entryway and slowly approached.

Mindy quaked in her pumps and craned her neck to look at him.

"You lost?" he asked.

It took her a moment to find her voice. "N-n-no. A friend told me about this place. She thought I-I-I'd like it."

One dark brow rose as he stared at her clothing. He didn't believe her. "What exactly did your friend tell you?"

Mindy's confidence wavered. Sweat laced her palms. She rubbed her hands along her skirt and swallowed hard. "Just that Sticks was a fun place." Her voice cracked.

He stared for a moment more, then shrugged. "Let me see your ID."

Mindy retrieved her license from her purse. Her fingers shook as she handed it to him. He sniffed, then returned her ID. The man settled back onto his stool and took out a stamp.

"How much is the cover charge?" she asked.

"Hold out your hand," he said.

She did as he asked.

He stamped a glowing wolf paw beneath her knuckles. "Have fun." The cheerful sentiment was ruined by his anxious expression.

"Thank you." Mindy put her license in her purse and stepped through the door. Her legs quivered when she saw the worn tables scattered around the room and sawdust on the floor. On the other side of the dance floor, a band was setting up their equipment.

Mindy tugged at her skirt again and waited for someone to greet her. After a minute, it was obvious no one was coming to show her to a table.

The music was louder now. It pumped out of the speakers, occupying the crowd until the live band started. The beat called to her, trying to lure her to the dance floor.

Mindy glanced around the bar. The place was packed and *exactly* like Celina described it. There were at least ten men for every woman in the bar, and most were exceedingly good-looking, especially the dark-haired, tattooed Adonis behind the bar. He was so gorgeous that he bordered on being pretty.

He smiled at Mindy and her knees went weak. She'd never be able to handle a man like him. Not in her wildest dreams, but flirting with the bartender never hurt.

She took a step forward and several heads turned in her direction. Mindy looked behind her, but there was no one there. The men sniffed in unison. She resisted the urge to do the same. She'd showered after work and put on a little perfume, but not too much. Or at least she'd thought so until she came in here.

Two guys broke away from the pack. Mindy giggled nervously at the metaphor, though it was fitting given the large group. They quickly approached her.

"Hello," the brown-haired one said. "My name's Marco. Marco Faretti. This here is Emmett."

"Hi. I'm Mindy." Every eye in the place was focused on

them.

"You look like you could use a drink," Marco said.

Her hands trembled as she smoothed her dress. "Yes, I could." Mindy let them drag her to the bar. She had no intention of staying there long. Not with the music calling to her.

They passed a man with sandy brown hair and haunting dark blue eyes that she hadn't noticed when she'd first walked in. Though how she could've missed him was a mystery. He leaned against the bar casually watching everyone around him, including her.

Like the doorman and bartender, the man was big and unusually tall. His rugged good looks were understated, but striking.

The man smiled at her. The act transformed his face and stole the breath from her lungs. Marco and Emmett faded away, along with the rest of the bar. Mindy smiled back, hoping her nerves didn't show.

Outwardly the man appeared to be having a good time, but Mindy recognized lonely when she saw it. After all, it stared back at her every time she looked in the mirror.

His gaze stole across her, leaving heat in its wake.

Mindy's heart raced. It had been a long time since she'd experienced that kind of attraction to a man.

Emmett put his arm around her.

The move shocked Mindy, breaking the spell between them. She casually shifted until his arm dropped. Maybe he wouldn't notice.

Undeterred, Emmett did it again.

This time Mindy looked at him before lifting his hand and removing his arm from around her shoulders. She didn't want the man at the end of the bar to get the wrong impression, and she didn't want to encourage Emmett.

Just because he and Marco had approached her first didn't mean that they had dibs on her. No one had dibs on her. Mindy wanted to make that clear upfront. She was grateful that they'd been so nice, but her gratitude only went so far.

The man at the end of the bar continued to watch her. Without warning, he suddenly came to his feet and rounded the bar. His gaze never wavered as he made his way toward her.

Mindy took a deep breath to calm her nerves. In her mind, she ran through a dozen ways of how to say hello. Before she could put any of them into practice, his footsteps faltered and he stopped. His disarming smile slowly faded and he returned to his spot at the end of the bar.

What just happened? Had I inadvertently done something? Had Emmett's clumsy attempt to hit on me dissuaded the man?

The disappointment swirling inside surprised Mindy. She glanced at her clothes and wished once more that she'd worn something casual. This wouldn't have happened to Celina or Isabel. They both had the ability to wrap men around their fingers.

Game playing of any kind gave Mindy hives. She'd always been a "what you see is what you get" kind of girl, and she'd been okay with that until tonight. Now Mindy wished just once that she were someone different. The kind of woman that the man at the end of the bar wouldn't be able to resist. The kind of woman who was brave enough to approach him without throwing up on his shoes.

If only I were that kind of woman... Mindy sighed.

The music changed to a more up-tempo beat. Mindy slipped away from Marco and Emmett, away from the man at the end of the bar, and away from her troubles.

She strolled out onto the dance floor, where a few other girls were already dancing. Mindy allowed the music to seep inside her, until she could feel every note pulsing in her bones. Her body swayed gently at first, then found the rhythm.

When was the last time she felt this free?

Mindy couldn't remember. Didn't care. She let the music wash over her and move her body. Her hips swayed and she ran her hands down her sides as she rocked to the beat.

* * * * *

Nic couldn't tear his gaze away from the woman in red as she swayed provocatively on the dance floor. That vintage dress she wore accentuated her voluptuous curves and fair skin, making her appear luminous in the low lighting. Her fluid movements hinted at the passion she kept buttoned up behind that high collar.

She looked young—innocent, but he'd never been good at guessing anyone's true age. The woman rolled her hips and ran her hands over her body.

Drool formed in his mouth. Nic had to swallow hard to keep from embarrassing himself. Every muscle in his body tightened and his skin burned. He reminded himself again that this woman was human and not one of the Kin.

Nic watched her dance until the song ended. He was awash with disappointment when she slowly strolled back to the bar, back to the pups who'd been nipping at her cute kitten heels.

* * * * *

Mindy made her way back to the bar and ordered a wine spritzer.

"Nice dance," the striking bartender said, then grinned.

"Thanks," she said, but Mindy hadn't danced for him or anyone else. That dance had been for her.

The bartender quickly made her drink, then placed the cocktail in front of her. "If you need anything else, just ask for Lucien," he said.

She smiled and gave him a quick nod.

A moment later, Lucien added five more drinks to go

with the first.

"I didn't order these," she said.

He looked at her, his green eyes mesmerizing. "I know, *jolie femme*. They did." Lucien indicated to the men behind her.

"Oh." Mindy reached into her purse for her money.

Lucien stopped her with a light touch to her hand. "It's already covered."

A growl came from the end of the bar. Mindy turned to see who'd made the odd noise, and so did everyone else at the bar. The sandy-haired man she'd been attracted to earlier was staring at the bartender's hand with a mutinous expression on his face.

"Well now, that is interesting," the bartender said, slowly removing his hand from hers.

"Did he just growl?" Mindy asked. She couldn't have heard him correctly. People didn't growl.

The bartender blinked. It was the only indication she got that let her know that she'd surprised him with the question.

"I mean no offense when I say this," Lucien said. "But I think perhaps you're in the wrong establishment."

Mindy thought the same thing, but stubbornness kept her rooted in place. Isabel wasn't the only one in her family capable of having a good time. She was determined to prove to her sister, to Celina, and to herself that some part of the "real" Mindy still existed. All she needed was the chance.

"I wish people would stop saying that," she murmured.

Why did everyone think they knew what was best for me? She wasn't a child. She was twenty-five years old.

With a grim expression on his lovely face, he gave her a slight bow. "As you wish."

* * * * *

Nic watched the woman order a drink. Sparks flew as she and Lucien spoke. The attraction between them was undeniable. Almost as strong as what they'd experienced before he discovered what she was. Lucien touched her lightly. Nic's wolf grumbled before he could stop it.

Everyone turned to look at him with shocked expressions on their faces. Everyone but Lucien. His best friend was having a hard time keeping a straight face.

Lucien said something to the woman, then walked to the end of the bar where Nic stood. "It's nice to know that there's still some life in you, *mon ami*. I was beginning to wonder." Speculation replaced some of his amusement.

"Funny," Nic said. "What can you tell me about her?"

Why had he asked? He didn't want to know her, didn't want anything to do with her. He wasn't looking to hook up with a human, even one as delectable as her.

Lucien cocked his hip against the bar. "Not much," he said. "Just that she doesn't belong here."

CHAPTER FOUR

The alcohol continued to flow, giving the men circling around Mindy liquid courage. She nursed her wine spritzer and danced alone a few more times.

The men grew more brazen. Marco and Emmett were determined to get her drunk and weren't above showing their displeasure over the fact that she hadn't touched the other drinks in front of her.

The man at the end of the bar continued to stare at her, but it was obvious he wasn't going to act upon their attraction. He'd made that perfectly clear. Once again, Mindy thought about approaching him, but the idea abandoned her when she noted his grim expression.

She'd never been good at reading people, only animals. People were complicated. Animals' needs were simple. It was why she'd gone into veterinary medicine.

Sticks continued to fill with people. The press of warm bodies around her made it hard to breathe. Emmett and Marco had been competing for the past hour to see who could get her to agree to a date. They were both beyond cute. Too bad they weren't her type. Deflecting their constant advances wore on her, and eventually she'd had enough.

Mindy pushed the last of her drink away and stood. She couldn't take it anymore. Celina was right. This wasn't her type of place. She waved goodbye to Lucien, then stepped away from the bar.

"Excuse me," she said to Marco and Emmett when she squeezed by.

"The bathrooms are down the hall on the right," Marco said.

"Thanks," Mindy said. "But I think I'm just going to head home. It was nice meeting you both."

"Don't go," Marco said. "You just got here."

Mindy glanced at her watch. She'd been there for over an hour. To a homebody, that felt like an eternity. "It's late and I have to work tomorrow. Thank you again for the drink." She didn't wait for them to respond. Mindy simply pushed past them and walked away.

She took a deep breath when she got outside. The air filled her lungs and cooled her heated skin. Mindy toddled across the parking lot toward her car. Her PJs and slippers were calling to her. Maybe she'd manage to get in an hour of studying before she went to bed.

"You're such a coward," she muttered. "You should've at least walked up to him and said hello."

It was too late now. She'd probably never see the man at the end of the bar again. Mindy was so lost in thought that she didn't hear the footsteps coming up behind her until they were upon her.

Marco and Emmett suddenly appeared out of the dark. "W-what are you guys doing?" She looked around, hoping someone was nearby, but they were alone.

"We wanted to make sure you got to your car okay," Marco said.

"Yeah, it's dark. Anything could happen," Emmett added.

"Thanks, but I'm already here." She pointed behind her.

Undeterred, the men kept coming. Mindy backed up and

didn't stop until she hit her car. The second she touched the metal doorframe, the men caged her with their bodies.

"Guys, I told you that I have to go home."

"We thought you might be up for a private party. You know, just the three us." Marco ran his fingers along her arm.

Fear warred with anger. Was this kind of behavior why Izzy made Celina promise never to invite her to the bar? Ugh, she'd been so stupid. She should have listened to Celina and just stayed away.

"I think I'd better leave," she said.

Emmett moved in front of her door handle, cutting off her escape. "It's early," he said. "We won't keep you long. We can make it quick, so you can get home and have a good night's sleep."

"As appealing as that sounds, I'm not interested," Mindy said with as much sarcasm as she could muster. She could barely hear the words over her pounding heart.

Marco snorted. "If you weren't interested, you wouldn't have come here."

"I came here to dance," Mindy said. "Not to meet people."

"Come on, baby," Marco said. "Stop playing coy. Nobody comes to Sticks for the music."

"I do," Emmett said.

"Shut up," Marco said. "Nobody is talking to you." He ground himself against her so she could feel the bulge protruding from the front of his pants. "You'll have a good time. It'll almost be like dancing. Promise."

Emmett laughed. "At least it'll be memorable."

Marco met his gaze and smiled, then he licked the side of her neck.

Mindy opened her mouth to scream, but Marco clamped his hand over her lips.

"Shh," he said. "Save the screaming for later."

* * * * *

Nic was determined to finish his beer now that the woman in red had gone, but he couldn't shake the unease coursing through his veins.

He'd watched the pups follow her out. They could be just planning to party, but this close to the full moon there was a chance their hormones were overriding their good sense.

They wouldn't rape her. That crime brought an automatic death sentence from the pack. But they could become excessively aggressive while trying to convince her to do what they wanted.

He wasn't a white knight. And he certainly wasn't the type to rescue anyone. If a human came here looking for a good time with a Were, then who was he to interfere?

Nic swore under his breath and shoved his hand into his pocket to pull out some cash. He tossed the money onto the bar and waved goodbye to Lucien. His friend gave him a knowing smirk, then went right back to work.

He rushed out the door and headed through the parking lot. He didn't get far before he heard sounds of a struggle taking place. Nic bolted in the direction of the sound. He found the two pups clumsily groping the blonde and trying to convince her to go into the woods. Her brown eyes were wide with alarm and she stank of fear.

Fury overtook him and Nic growled low. So low that only the two Weres could hear him. Their heads whipped around to confront the threat. Matching sets of glowing eyes stared at him.

"Leave the lady alone," Nic said.

"Don't you have somewhere you need to be, old man?" the more daring of the two asked.

His friend shuffled his feet, putting some distance between him and the woman. Sweat broke out across his forehead and his Adam's apple convulsed in his throat.

At least one of them is smart, Nic thought.

Thirty wasn't exactly ancient, but he could see how a couple of twenty-somethings might think so. Nic didn't know these two, and they certainly didn't know him or they wouldn't be so mouthy.

"I'm not going to tell you again, *son*." Menace dripped from Nic's words.

"We're just having ourselves a good time. Aren't we, sweetheart?" The young pup grabbed the woman's arm, and she squeaked. "You need to move along before you get hurt."

At 230 pounds, Nic wasn't exactly a lightweight. Maybe the pup thought that since there were two of them that they could easily take him. It was a mistake they were going to regret. He might be naturally laidback, but he hadn't reached his position in the pack by being a pushover.

Nic's gaze shifted to the frightened woman. "Get in your car and get out of here."

She gave him a jerky nod and reached for her car door. The second she opened it, the young pup closest to her slammed the door shut. The woman flinched.

"You aren't going anywhere." His gaze never left Nic's as he spoke to her.

Nic shrugged. "Have it your way."

The pup farthest from the woman launched himself at Nic. Nic swung his fist, catching the pup under the chin. The Were flew through the air and landed on his butt. He shook his head, trying to clear it, and struggled to his feet.

Before he could right himself, the other Were attacked. His body slammed into Nic, taking them both to the ground. The pup got in a couple of good blows before Nic managed to throw him off.

Nic got to his feet, only to be punched in the face by the Were he'd taken down first. The blow caught him beneath the eye, slicing his skin open. Blood trickled over his face onto the front of his shirt. The next punch he dodged, but the pup's fist still managed to clip his ear. The move pissed him off.

"Enough!" Nic shouted, and tossed the pup at his friend. They collided, and both fell to the ground.

Nic faced the two young Weres, keeping his back to the woman. While he glared at them, he allowed a hint of his wolf to surface. The world turned to gray as his eyes shifted and his incisors lengthened. Power swept out in front of him, washing over them.

The two Weres paled and scrambled back.

"Go! Now!" The words came out garbled, but his meaning was clear.

"Come on," the smarter of the two said. He grabbed his friend's arm, dragging him away.

"This isn't finished," the brazen one shouted before he left.

Yes, it is, Nic thought.

* * * * *

Mindy never imagined that anyone would ever fight over her. "Cute" didn't inspire men to lay down their lives. Sure, she'd heard about fights happening and had seen them many times in the animal kingdom, when a male was fighting for the right to mate, but she'd never experienced it firsthand.

Celina had told her how thrilling the experience was. At the time, Mindy had thought Celina's need for constant drama and reassurance had led her to exaggerate, but she hadn't. At least not entirely.

Mindy couldn't deny the thrill skating along her spine or the sudden unwelcome surge of arousal. *What did that say about her?*

When her would-be savior had first arrived, Mindy wasn't sure if it was a good thing or if the situation had just gone from bad to worse. Now she had no doubt that he'd saved her life, or at least saved her from something truly unpleasant.

Her eyes were drawn to the play of muscles beneath his T-shirt as he watched the men who'd been hassling her leave. He was *magnificent*. Her gaze slowly lowered and the impressive view got even better.

Her heart continued to pound, but now it was from more than fear. And Mindy wasn't at all certain how she planned to handle that.

* * * * *

Between the impending full moon and the adrenaline pumping through him, Nic was having a difficult time maintaining a civilized façade.

Weres only fought over females for the opportunity to mate. His body hardened as bone-deep instincts attempted to arrest his control. Nic clamped down hard on his feral nature.

The breeze shifted, bringing her sweet scent to him. Sex was the last thing he wanted from a human—even one that smelled so delicious. He gritted his teeth and clenched his fists. He had to get his wolf leashed before he looked at her. His body was making demands that couldn't be met.

Nic decided his only recourse was to make sure she was okay, then leave before he did something they'd both regret. Nic took a deep breath and faced her, determined to get it over with. The second their eyes met, his resolve crumbled like clay in the hot sun.

CHAPTER FIVE

Mindy was used to dealing with injured animals, not humans. So nothing could've prepared her for the jolt that struck the moment his dark blue eyes met hers.

Blood smeared his cheek and dust covered his shirt. There was something wild about his gaze, something utterly untamed. It drew her in when every instinct screamed at her to escape.

Mindy couldn't leave him. Not like this. Not after he'd fought to protect her. She pushed away from the car and tried to touch him.

"Don't!" The single word was torn from his chest as he grabbed her wrist. His hard, unyielding grip bordered on painful.

"You're hurt." She hesitated, then pressed on, drawn to the heat simmering in his eyes. The moment her fingers made contact with his taut face, the man groaned and pulled her into his arms.

His lips came down upon hers before Mindy could take a breath. He kissed her with such stark hunger that her body immediately went up in flames. The wildness inside her that had been dormant for so long flared to life and pushed aside all logic.

Mindy's body melted into his hard chest. Just for tonight, she didn't want to be the responsible sibling. She wanted to be someone other than "Monotonous Mindy." She wanted to be...herself for once.

She didn't notice that he'd released her arm until she'd wrapped her hands around his neck and sunk her fingers into his soft hair. By then it was too late to pull back.

* * * * *

Alarm bells rang in Nic's head. He immediately hit snooze and kept kissing her. He couldn't get enough of her sweet taste. He'd been prepared to let her walk away. Planned to make her leave. Then she'd gone and done the unthinkable. She'd touched him.

The heat from her fingertips incinerated his good intentions, sending them up in smoke. Nic pulled her into his arms and kissed her.

For one insane moment, he worried that he was no better than the Weres who'd been trying to take advantage of her. The thought unraveled when her blunt teeth sank into his lower lip and she ran her tongue across the tender bite.

Nic shuddered and his big body jerked, then his hands locked tighter around her. He kneaded her round bottom, then cupped her and lifted her off her feet. She fit perfectly in his hands, as if she were made for him. The thought ratcheted up his need, and Nic grew harder.

Despite her petite size and her vintage dress, the woman managed to wrap her legs around his hips. Nic groaned into her mouth as the ridge of his maleness collided with her feminine heat. If he didn't get inside her soon, his head would explode.

He carried her away from her car, away from the entrance to Sticks, to his pick-up truck. They were near enough to the tree line and far enough from the bar to ensure a level of privacy they wouldn't otherwise have. Still, Nic scanned the area with his acute senses to ensure they were alone before lowering his tailgate and setting her down upon it.

One hand continued to massage her lush bottom, while the other reached under her dress. He willed himself to slow, let them catch their breath and allow good sense to return, but he couldn't. It was like he was being driven by an unseen force that was determined to take, to seize.

Nic chalked his urgency up to the moon's influence, though he couldn't recall this ever happening before. His exploring fingers encountered lace, then struck moisture and scalding heat.

Just one taste. That was all he wanted. That's all he needed. He pulled his hand out and licked the moisture off his fingers.

Her taste burst over his tongue and he nearly dropped to his knees. Overwhelmed by the sensations, Nic growled in the back of his throat. He'd never tasted anything like her. So rich, so creamy, so addictively delicious.

Nic needed more. He hiked her skirt up and ripped her panties off. "I'll buy you new ones," he rasped, as her feminine musk surrounded them.

The heady aroma betrayed her eagerness. It also fueled the fire roaring through his veins. Nic's lips found hers once more.

He wanted to bury his nose between her thighs. Wanted to lick her depths until she quivered beneath him, begging him to take her, but Nic couldn't wait—and neither could she, if the needy whimpers coming from her throat were any indication.

He deepened the kiss, swirling his tongue around her mouth, trying to capture her essence. Each did their best to devour the other.

The woman pulled at his shirt and ran her fingers along his back, then grasped his ass and yanked him closer.

Her petals unfurled for him as he sank his fingers into her

scalding heat. She instantly tightened around him. Nic waited a heartbeat, then added another finger and continued his intimate exploration. She felt like heaven and smelled like candy-coated sin. Nic couldn't get enough of her.

With a twist of his hand, he found her swollen flesh. He stroked the tender nub, driving her higher, leaving her teetering on the edge of oblivion.

"Please," she gasped.

Her begging didn't sit well with him. If anything, he should be the one groveling at her feet. Nic reached into his back pocket and pulled out a condom. He couldn't catch any human diseases, and one sniff told him that she was disease free. There was no chance he could get her pregnant. Weres could only procreate with their bondmates, and even then, they had to be marked. But the prophylactic would ease her mind.

Nic ignored the ache in his jaw and focused on the one in his pants. He popped the button on his jeans and his zipper hissed as he eased it down. Her hands were on him in an instant, taking his breath and making him weak. Nic gritted his teeth and prayed for strength to hold out long enough to get the condom on.

* * * * *

Mindy's body was on fire. She'd never been this brazen in her life. She'd also never wanted a man this much. If she weren't in total control of her faculties, Mindy would swear she'd been possessed. She had never understood what made sex such an all-consuming big deal—until now.

She pulled back from their kiss and saw him sheathe himself. His immense size obviously extended to every part of his body. For one crazy minute, she didn't think this would be anatomically possible.

"Wait!" Mindy held her hand against his chest as he positioned the thick head at her entrance. Was she really going to do this? Was this really her?

He clenched his jaw and his big body trembled, but her savior stopped instantly. "Have you changed your mind?" he asked, his expression pained.

Had she? Mindy stared into his dark blue eyes and found herself falling once more. No, she wanted this. Wanted him. Had from the moment she'd laid eyes on him. If only for tonight, she'd have him and be the kind of woman she'd always known she could be.

"No." Mindy shook her head. "Just needed to catch my breath."

"Thank the moon!" he said, then seized her mouth once more.

Mindy's thoughts scattered to the stars as he sent her sailing across a sea of pure sensation. He brushed her entrance, then ran himself up and down her moist cleft. Once he was covered in her juices, he pulled back and thrust forward, impaling her.

* * * * *

Nic swallowed her shocked cry, then tried to catch his breath as his body adjusted to the vise-like hold she had on it. He wasn't a small man, but he hadn't expected her to be quite so tight. Nic quivered as he tried to hold himself still inside her pulsing core.

For a moment, he'd thought she was a virgin and his heart had nearly stopped. She wasn't, but the woman was blissfully snug. Snug enough to let him know that it had been a while since she'd had a man inside her.

The realization left him feeling ridiculously pleased. He kissed her gently and slowly sucked on the tip of her tongue, savoring her passion, while he waited for her to relax.

Her body's grip on him eventually eased. Nic carefully rocked his hips to test her readiness.

She whimpered, then sighed.

The woman melted around him, while her big brown eyes shimmered with desire. Nic found himself drowning in their chocolaty depths, wanting to spend eternity there. All sense of self-preservation went out the window.

Lost in her eyes, he thrust again, gliding smoothly into her. She sank her fingernails into his forearms and tugged. Nic dropped onto his elbows. The move crushed the ripe swell of her breasts against his unyielding chest. Her nipples beaded instantly.

Nic pulled his mouth away from hers and nibbled on her earlobe. She hooked her ankles around him and canted her hips. He slipped further into her. Nic shuddered. The ache in his jaw returned with a vengeance and his lips automatically strayed to her delicate neck.

Her erratic pulse jumped beneath his lips. She was so soft, so sweet...so perfect. He licked the spot where her neck and shoulder met. The taste of her intensified and changed.

Nic's incisors lengthened. The urge to bite her was so strong that it burned through his soul.

Do it! an insidious voice whispered.

Nic jerked his head away.

His wolf snarled.

What was wrong with his beast? It shouldn't be doing that. It shouldn't *want* to do that. He couldn't believe how easy it had been to let his wolf take control and to forget that she was human.

The woman writhed beneath him. His lips found her pebbled nipples through her dress and he sucked hard. Nic wanted to bare her for his greedy eyes to feast upon, taste what his senses detected, but there wasn't time. It was far too dangerous with his control so tenuous.

His hands latched on to her full hips and he picked up speed. The first ripple struck. She sobbed and her body clamped down on him. The urgency inside of Nic grew. He couldn't seem to get deep enough or move fast enough to satiate his beast. Then, the unthinkable happened...

Nic began to *swell*.

At first he was too stunned to react, convinced he was mistaken. Once the shock wore off, panic struck. Nic tried to pull out, but he it was too late. His body had already locked with hers. He couldn't budge more than an inch in either direction.

"No!" he shouted, as the first of his orgasms struck, blinding him with passion.

Somewhere in the distance, Nic heard his wolf bark with laughter.

* * * * *

He was everywhere.

Mindy had no idea she could be so *full* and so hungry at the same time. His body blanketed hers, blocking out the stars. What they were doing was insane. She was insane, but Mindy couldn't bring herself to feel an ounce of regret. She couldn't manage anything beyond the searing pleasure he was giving her.

He surged forward, burying himself deep, and expanded inside her. The tremors that started a moment ago increased. The delicious shudders turned into quakes as her body erupted.

His hands latched on to her hips and he ground himself into her.

Mindy's back bowed off the truck bed as something exploded inside of her. She couldn't see, couldn't hear anything but the blood roaring in her ears.

He grunted and doubled his efforts. He wasn't thrusting as deeply as before, but he continued to ride her body like the hounds of hell were nipping at his heels.

He drove Mindy headfirst into another shattering release. As she tumbled over the edge into oblivion, she heard him bellow.

The sound morphed into something primal, almost

animalistic. It made her ears ring, but Mindy didn't care. She was pretty sure she'd just died and gone to heaven.

Chapter Six

Nic wasn't sure what just happened. One minute he'd been so lost inside her that the world had disappeared and the next his wolf had taken over. How long had they been lying here locked together?

No, not locked together. Not anymore. He could move again. What was he going to do? How could he explain that this should never have happened—had never happened before—when he didn't understand himself?

Nic expected to see contempt and accusation. At the very least confusion over what had occurred, since it wasn't every day a human experienced such a thing. But none of those emotions were visible. Instead, acceptance greeted him.

How could she feel that way after what he'd just done to her? Her selflessness only added to his sense of guilt. Nic took a moment to study her.

Her swollen lips, sleepy brown eyes, and mussed blonde hair made her look like a woman who'd been well loved. The sight of her stole the breath from his lungs.

She couldn't be the one. She just couldn't be. It wasn't possible.

He needed to think. Needed to get away from her to clear

his head. Nic didn't trust himself. Didn't trust his wolf. He wasn't convinced any of this was real.

The woman stirred beneath him.

Nic took a choppy breath and pushed himself up. "You okay?" he asked, hoping his voice sounded steady.

Color flooded her face, matching her wrinkled red dress. She nodded. "That was amazing."

More like life altering, he thought, but didn't say so.

The sound of gravel crunching and music pounding came rushing at him. He remembered where they were and why they were here. They were still alone, but wouldn't be for long. Shame warred with embarrassment, but neither could contend with the confusion running rampant through him.

"I'm sorry," he murmured, and slipped out of her.

Nic helped the woman up so she could straighten her clothes. While she did that, he removed the condom and pulled his jeans up. He shoved the used latex into his pocket.

The woman buried her face in her hands. "I can't believe we did that here of all places. Anyone could've wandered by."

Nic wanted to reassure her that that wouldn't have happened, but he couldn't. The second he'd entered her, he'd been gone. Her body had transported him to another world. A world that felt dangerously like home. A world he didn't dare trust. He ran a shaky hand through his hair.

"I-" The word tangled in his throat.

"You don't have to apologize. You don't have to say anything. We're both adults. I'm just as guilty of poor judgment here as you are," she said.

She took a step and wobbled. Nic instinctively reached out to steady her, and the heat that had engulfed them reignited. He dropped his hand and asked for her keys. She handed them to him.

Nic walked her back to her car and opened the door. Out of habit, he climbed in and started the engine for her. The car sputtered to life, then immediately made a pinging noise.

He frowned. "How long has it been doing that?" Nic asked.

"A while," she said, unable to meet his gaze. "I'll get it taken care of."

He opened his mouth to offer to fix it for her, but closed it when he saw her mottled face. Nic climbed out and waited for her to slip behind the wheel.

There was no sense dragging the awkward moment out. It was obvious what this was. Anything else was a fluke of the moon. So why did he find himself lingering next to her door, reluctant to see her leave?

The wind shifted, carrying with it an all-too- familiar scent. Nic stiffened and slowly scanned the woods. He didn't spot the two pups, but they were there. Somewhere. How long had they been there? Had they been watching the whole time?

No! He shook his head. He would've known.

Something vicious snarled inside him and raised its furry head. It didn't want other Weres anywhere near her. Nic refused to look too closely at why.

"Drive safely," he said, and stepped back so she could leave.

* * * * *

Mindy was startled by his sudden change in demeanor. She could've sworn he'd been about to ask for her number or say something more. Why had he changed his mind? Did it matter? Her confidence seeped away as the wildness she'd experienced a moment ago deserted her.

"Um—thanks," she stuttered.

For a split second, his blue eyes glowed as he stared at her, but in a blink the light was gone.

"You don't have to thank me," he said, sounding tired.

"I guess this is goodbye." Her tone reeked of desperation. *Go! Now! Before you embarrass yourself even more.*

56

Mindy threw her car into gear and backed up. She needed to get out of here. Get away from Sticks. Get away from him.

He stood rooted in place as she drove away. The second she could no longer see him, something inside of her cracked and tears welled in her eyes. She stopped and banged her forehead on the steering wheel.

"Stupid. Stupid. Stupid," she muttered, then continued on.

Mindy replayed the events of the evening the whole drive home. She was sure the man had enjoyed himself as much as she had. Maybe more so. She rolled her eyes. Of course he'd enjoyed himself. He was guy who was getting laid. Except...it had felt like more than just sex to her.

She was aware that women and men viewed these things differently, but no matter how many times she examined what they'd done, she couldn't easily dismiss the connection she'd felt with...with...

Mindy sighed. Oh God, she didn't even know his name. Shame kicked her in the gut, leaving her winded. How could she have forgotten to ask something so important? She thought about turning around.

She glanced in her rearview mirror. The road behind her was dark and empty. It matched the hollowness in her chest. It was too late to go back now. He'd be long gone.

All this time, she'd envied Izzy's and Celina's wild streaks because she'd had to suppress her own. Mindy had finally let her wild side out, only to discover it wasn't what it was cracked up to be.

Sure, she'd enjoyed every minute with her mystery man and wouldn't trade the experience for anything. But Celina and Izzy had left something out of their adventurous tales. Something vital.

They'd forgot to mention how quickly the momentary highs would be replaced by crushing lows. The sharp edges of which only added to her sense of loneliness.

* * * * *

Nic arrived home to an empty house. The silence screamed volumes as he dropped his keys into a bowl next to the door and stripped off his clothes.

His chest ached. Nic rubbed the spot over his heart, but the pain remained. Didn't seem possible, but he was even lonelier than before.

The woman's sweet scent covered his body, making his heart race and his nerves tighten. He could still feel her velvet muscles gripping him and taste her honey on his tongue. He stared at the hard evidence protruding between his legs. He could deny it, but here was physical proof that he wanted her again.

Nic walked into the bathroom and turned the shower on, determined to wash her scent away—*wash her away*. He stared at the steady stream and watched it swirl down the drain. One quick scrub and she'd be gone.

For some reason, he couldn't bring himself to step under the water. Having her scent on him made it seem like he wasn't so alone.

"You don't even know her name," he snapped, overwhelmed by the sense of loss.

Nic shut the water off and walked to the sink. Clutching the sides of the porcelain, he stared at himself in the mirror. Blue phosphorescent eyes stared back at him accusingly and dried blood covered his face.

"You're wrong," he grumbled to his wolf.

His lip curled, exposing long canines.

"You've been wrong before and you're wrong this time! It's just the full moon." The words had barely left his throat, when Nic's head snapped back.

Fur rippled over his face and a snout appeared. His skin itched and stretched. Nic growled and shook his head, fighting off the need to complete the shift.

"You aren't in control. I am!" The garbled words ended in a snarl.

It took a couple of minutes for the fur and snout to slowly recede. By the time it was completely gone, the cut on his cheek had sealed and only a thin white line remained. That too would disappear in another day or so.

Nic washed his face and brushed his teeth, then went to bed. His skin smelled of her. The heady aroma was both ecstasy and sheer torture, but he needed it to get through the night.

CHAPTER SEVEN

Celina turned the television off when Slade stalked into the apartment. Every time she saw him, he made her breath catch and her heart skip a beat.

With his dark hair, tanned skin, and ridiculously long lashes, he bordered on beautiful. The sharp edge of his cheekbones and square thrust of his jaw kept the distinction at bay.

She glanced at the time. After midnight—again. "Where have you been?"

Slade looked at her, but there was no heat in his amber eyes. "Out."

"I made you dinner." She pointed to the cling-film-covered plate on the table. "It's probably cold by now."

The muscles of his broad shoulders rolled as he shrugged. "I already ate," he said, but sniffed the food anyway.

Celina rose from the couch and wrapped her arms around his trim waist. "What's wrong?"

"Nothing," he said, then tried to shake her off.

But Celina wasn't having it. She tightened her grip and clung to him. "You can tell me anything," she said.

Slade growled. "I said it's nothing."

Celina instantly released him. She could feel him pulling away emotionally and had no idea how to stop it. When she'd first brought him home from the clinic a week and a half ago, Slade had been grateful.

He'd wanted to know all about Breakbend and the culture. He'd watched tons of television and spent hours on the internet. It made her think he'd never seen it before, which wasn't possible unless he'd been living under a rock.

She'd helped him with everything she could given her limited resources. Afterward, Slade had been grateful. Grateful enough to sleep with her. He'd even hinted at them having a future together. The thought that that future might be slipping away terrified her.

Izzy's cryptic warning echoed in her head. Celina pushed it aside. Her best friend may be psychic, but she didn't know everything. If she'd ever experienced the passion inside a Were, she wouldn't be so quick to avoid them or so quick to judge.

"What can you tell me about the Moonlight Kin in the area?" Slade asked.

Celina blinked in surprise. "Not much. I'm sure you know more than I do, since you're one of them."

Slade glanced at her. "I'm not part of *this* group."

"Oh," she said. "I just thought..."

Impatience simmered in his amber gaze.

"What do you need to know?" An inkling of unease trickled down her spine. If he wasn't part of the Moonlight Kin, that meant he was trespassing on their territory. Wolves were extremely territorial. If the Kin detected Slade, he would be in danger.

"Is it normal for the Kin to run by Telegraph Road?" he asked.

Mindy lived on Telegraph Road. Hers was one of the few houses out that way. She'd got it for her and Izzy because the rent was cheap and she could keep as many animals there as she wanted.

What was Slade doing out there?

"It doesn't matter what I was doing. Just answer the question," he said.

Celina's stomach dropped to the floor. *Did he just read my thoughts?* She'd never heard of a Were who could do that. The idea was horrifying. Fear cooled her ardor.

"I'm pretty sure the Moonlight Kin only run on Aidan Fortier's estate," she said.

"Is he the Alpha?" Slade asked.

"Yes," she said, then amended her answer: "I think so. I've never met him."

"No surprise there. Alphas are *particular* about the female company they keep," he said.

It took her a beat to catch the insult. Celina stiffened. "What exactly do you mean by that?"

Slade smiled and kissed her cheek. "Nothing, sweetheart."

Celina wanted him—wanted this—so bad that she was willing to put up with a lot. That would change once they were mated.

A smile ghosted Slade's face as he pulled off his shirt and dropped it onto the arm of the couch. Her eyes devoured every inch of his bare skin. Celina had never seen a man built like him. He sported so many hard ridges and shadowed lines that he didn't look real.

His long, tapered fingers moved to the button on the front of his jeans. She'd had those fingers inside every orifice and still she wanted more, needed more.

Slade popped the button. The denim slipped an inch, riding low on his hips, exposing the indentations that hinted at greater perfection. He didn't seem to notice her physical response. Without a second glance, he walked into the bedroom.

Celina tried not to drool as she watched him go. The second he was out of sight, she glanced at the phone and debated whether to call Mindy.

And say what? Be careful, werewolves are sniffing around your house? Watch out, werewolves are real? She'd have her committed.

"Celina," Slade's raspy voice called out.

She recognized the tone immediately. He only sounded sexy like that when he wanted some, wanted her. The realization dispersed her doubts and bolstered her hopes.

"What, babe?" she asked.

"I'm hungry," he said, surprising her.

Celina glanced at the food on the table. "You want me to heat up the plate?"

"I don't want food," he said. "I want you to get your butt in here and take your clothes off."

Desire mingled with defeat. Celina couldn't resist his call, hadn't been able to from the start. Slade had come into her life and stolen her soul.

No, not stolen, she thought. She'd given it to him willingly. Wrapped it in a bow and handed her soul over, along with her self-respect.

Celina reached for the bottom of her T-shirt and pulled it over her head. She hadn't bothered to put on a bra, since Slade didn't like them. He wanted easy and fast access. She dropped the shirt onto the floor and slowly strolled into the bedroom.

Slade was lying on top of her white comforter with his back pressed against the wrought-iron headboard. He was gloriously naked, waiting for her. His tight fist encased his swollen flesh, emphasizing his arousal.

Celina gulped, drinking in the sight of him. He was big and thick. Everything about him was sheer perfection. "You're beautiful."

He ignored the compliment as if it were his due. "About time," he said, stroking himself. "This isn't going to suck itself."

Celina let out a desperate whimper and dropped to her knees.

"That's a good girl," Slade said, as she brushed his hands aside and grasped him, then slowly lowered her head.

Chapter Eight

The sun had barely peeked its golden head above the horizon, when Nic arrived at work the next morning. He punched in his security code and the large metal gate swung open. Nic pulled through and stopped, waiting for the gate to close behind him.

They'd had a security breach not long ago. Jenna Dane's "ex" had broken onto the estate and threatened to expose the Kin.

The problem had been dealt with swiftly, but he and the other wolves had become more vigilant about the pack's security.

The woods rushed by as Nic meandered down the long drive. The concrete and stone manor came into view as the trees parted and the road split in two. If he veered right, he'd go toward the circular drive in front of the house.

He went left. Most of Aidan's estate was still asleep, but the lights were on in the garage as he pulled his truck up and parked.

Nic walked in to find Josh Dubois and Bernie Macklemore already hard at work.

"Morning," Nic said, and went straight for the pot of

coffee on the shelf.

Josh popped his dark head out from beneath the hood of the sports car he was working on. He was a wiry twenty-something who laughed as much as he talked and had the kind of energy that would shame that battery- operated bunny. "You look like crap. Must've been some night." Josh grinned and his youthful eyes danced with glee.

Bernie slid out from under the sedan he'd been adjusting and hauled himself to his feet with a groan. He looked to be a fit fifty thanks to his shifter genes, but was in all likelihood double that age. Methodical and wise, Bernie considered each word before he spoke. His gaze landed on Nic and his gray brow arched. "What happened to you?"

"Nothing." Nic avoided his gaze. "Had a little scuffle last night with some pups who were out to test their claws."

Josh laughed. "They aren't very bright if they decided to tangle with you."

Nic laughed. "They weren't," he said.

"Want me to talk to them?" Josh asked.

Nic shook his head. "They don't live here on the estate. I've never seen them before. Must be out-of- towners in for the full-moon run."

Bernie's eyes narrowed, but he said nothing.

Nic walked to the truck he'd been working on yesterday and set his coffee down on the floor, then slipped under the vehicle. He reached for a wrench to loosen the bolts. The wrench slipped from his fingers and dropped onto the floor with a loud clang. He picked it up, only to drop it again.

The third time the wrench hit the concrete, Bernie and Josh quit working on their cars and came to see if he needed a hand.

"Doing okay?" Bernie asked.

"Fine," Nic said through gritted teeth. He twisted the wrench and scraped a layer of skin off his knuckles.

Josh sniffed. "Ah, Nic, he said. "I don't mean to pry, but when did you start wearing women's perfume?"

Nic banged his head on the undercarriage. He muttered a curse, then slid out from under the truck. He rolled to his feet and walked to the neatly arranged wall of tools on the far side of the garage.

Bernie followed him. "Want to talk about it?"

Nic didn't look at him. Instead, he continued to examine the tools. "Nothing to talk about."

Bernie cocked his head. "If it's nothing, then where'd the perfume come from?"

Nic shrugged and kept his expression neutral. "Just a girl I picked up at the bar last night."

"She have anything to do with the scuffle?" Bernie asked.

Nic didn't answer.

Bernie stared at him for a solid minute.

Nic fought the urge to squirm.

"What's her name?" Bernie asked.

Nic's face heated. "Don't know. Doesn't matter."

"You don't know her name?" Bernie took a deep breath and slowly let it out. "How long have I known you?"

Nic looked at him in surprise. "What?"

"How long have we known each other?" Bernie asked.

Nic thought about it. "Ten years, give or take."

Bernie nodded. "Sounds right," he said. "In all that time, I can't recall you ever coming to work smelling like a girl you picked up at a bar."

Nic turned away, but Bernie caught his sleeve. He looked down at the hand and snarled.

Bernie's brow disappeared into his hairline. "Okay, now that we've established that she's not just some nameless girl you picked up at a bar, it's time to talk. Take a seat." He pointed to a stool in the corner of the garage. "Josh, run to the main house and get me a pastry."

"Nic, you want anything?" Josh asked.

"No thanks!"

The younger man nodded and strode out the door.

As soon as he was gone, Bernie leveled his gaze on Nic.

"Now tell me what happened."

"I already told you," Nic said. "I got into with some pups and hooked up with a girl afterwards."

"You aren't a hookup kind of guy," Bernie said.

"Sure I am."

"No." Bernie shook his head. "You're not," he said patiently.

Nic shrugged. "I was last night."

"Hmm...interesting." Bernie got himself a cup of coffee. He made a show of taking a sip, then returned to Nic's side. "So let me make sure I have this right. You got into a fight—that may or may not involve a woman—then picked up some random bar girl to have sex with and didn't bother to ask her name."

"That about sums it up," Nic said. His jaw hurt from gritting his teeth so hard.

"I'm confused," Bernie said. "If it was such a fun night, and you certainly smell like it was, then why are you so grumpy?"

"I'm not grumpy," Nic snapped.

Bernie watched him closely. "You got into a fight. Found an easy lay. Sounds like a Were's idea of a perfect night."

"She wasn't easy," Nic said. She hadn't been with a man in a while. He was sure of that. Just the thought of her lying with another guy made Nic's head ache and claws flex.

Bernie scratched his chin. "You said she was a bar girl. If she was at Sticks, that makes her a Were groupie."

"I might have met her at the bar, but she was *not* a regular. Lucien didn't recognize her and she had no idea what I was," Nic ground out.

He didn't like that Bernie thought the woman was easy or that she was a groupie. She wasn't. Despite what they'd done in the parking lot, she was an innocent. Far too sweet for her own good.

"She didn't belong there. And she damn sure doesn't belong with me." Nic scrubbed a hand through his hair.

Bernie took another sip of his coffee. "I never said she did. It's interesting that you brought it up, though."

"Our beasts don't know everything," Nic growled. "They *can* be wrong."

"I've never known them to be, but I suppose anything is possible. We're proof of that." Bernie hid his smile behind his coffee cup.

"I need to get back to work," Nic snarled in frustration.

"Can I come back in now? I have your pastry." Josh poked his head in the door.

"Yes," Bernie said. "I've learned everything I needed to know."

Nic scowled at him.

"Jenna has a question." Josh set the pastry on the workbench.

"What does she want to know?" Bernie asked.

"I'll let her ask you herself," Josh said.

Nic didn't look up when Jenna Dane walked into the garage. His mind was too focused on the woman from last night. He'd been unable to think of anything else. Was she still sleeping? Or was she awake, regretting what they'd done?

Part of him did. While a larger half would do it again in a heartbeat.

Even though the night hadn't gone as planned, Nic didn't want her to regret their time together. He scratched his jaw. His fingers encountered stubble. He needed a shave. He needed a shower, but he couldn't stand the thought of losing her scent. He heard muttering.

"What?" he asked. It was then that Nic noticed Jenna standing next to him, talking. How long had she been there?

Somehow she'd squeezed her pregnant body between the truck and the tray of tools beside it. Her strawberry- blonde curls fell loosely down her back. She was smiling and stroking her stomach while she waited for his response.

"I'm sorry, what did you want?" Nic asked.

Jenna's grin widened. "I asked when you thought the truck would be ready."

"Uh." He reached for a tool and knocked the whole tray onto the ground. Nic flushed. "Might be a while."

Jenna's light green eyes twinkled. "Looks like it," she said. "Don't worry about it. We can use the SUV."

"I can probably have it up and running by the end of the day," Nic said.

Jenna touched his arm. "No rush."

There was a time when her touch brought him nothing but pain. Now Nic didn't feel anything, and he had his one-night stand to thank for that. Too bad he didn't know her name and had no way of reaching her.

* * * * *

Jenna waddled out of the garage.

"Never thought I'd see the day you'd—"

Bernie hit Josh before he could finish the sentence.

Josh's brow furrowed and he looked at him. "What?"

Bernie shook his head in warning. He didn't want anything to spoil this moment. This was the first time Jenna had come into the garage and not left Nic tied up in knots.

He watched his friend slip back under the truck, totally unaware of what just occurred. Happiness filled him. It was about time the young wolf stopped obsessing over the Alpha's mate.

Bernie didn't know who Nic had met last night, but whoever she was, she'd changed his friend's life for the better. How long would it take him to figure that out and hunt her down? Hopefully not long. He wanted Nic to move back to the estate. Back home with the pack where he belonged.

* * * * *

Every time Nic inhaled, he smelled her honeyed scent and pictured her writhing beneath him. The aroma distracted him, but not half as much as the instant replay. He banged his thumb twice and lost count of how many times he'd dropped his tools.

After a few hours, he'd had enough. Nic needed to get some fresh air. Needed to clear his head. Needed to stop thinking about her, when there was a very good chance he'd never see her again.

His wolf surged to the surface and stared out through his eyes. It raised its furry head and sniffed the air. The woman's scent drifted deep into its lungs, then it sank back, hovering just beneath his skin.

He might be willing to walk away, but it wasn't.

"I'm going into town to grab some lunch." Nic headed for the door. "I'll pick up the cables we need while I'm there."

"The chef's putting on a big spread at the house. We don't need—"

Bernie hit Josh and glared at him. "See you in a few."

Nic nodded and strode outside. He climbed into his truck and started the engine. As he roared down the long drive toward the security gate, some of the tension in his chest eased.

* * * * *

Josh turned to Bernie after Nic left. "You want to tell me what's going on? I've never seen Nic so distracted. He didn't notice that Jenna was here."

"I know." Bernie grinned. "It's only going to get worse."

"What is?" Josh asked.

"Isn't it obvious?" Bernie replied.

Josh scratched his head. "Maybe to you." He grabbed the pastry and handed it to Bernie.

Bernie looked at it, sniffed, then wrinkled his nose. He

tossed the confection into the trash.

"You better not let the cook see you do that," Josh said. "He went to a lot of trouble to make those fresh. I thought you wanted a pastry."

"No, I just needed to talk to Nic," Bernie said. "I wanted to confirm my suspicions."

"What suspicions are those?" Josh asked.

"Our friend Nic has found his bondmate," Bernie said.

Josh's eyes widened and he glanced at the door Nic had walked out of. "Why didn't he say anything? It's such a big deal. Definitely cause for celebration."

Bernie cocked his head and his smile widened. "Because I don't think he knows. At least not for certain."

Josh grabbed his stomach and hooted with laughter. "Oh man," he said. "Can't wait to see Nic's face when he finally figures it out."

Bernie chuckled. "Should be something, all right. In the meantime, cut him some slack. His wolf will really be riding him hard until he closes the deal."

Chapter Nine

Celina cornered Mindy the second she walked into the animal clinic. "Did anything odd happen last night?"

The humiliation over what she'd done came rushing back. Mindy couldn't meet Celina's penetrating gaze. "W-what do mean?" She rushed past the cheery light blue walls with the doggy and kitty pictures on them, and slipped into the office.

Celina followed. "Slade's a catch. I get it," she said. "I know if I find him irresistible, it's a safe bet that other women do, too."

Mindy had no idea how Slade figured into last night. "What?"

"If he dropped by your house, you can tell me. I won't be mad." Pain filled her eyes and she squared her shoulders.

"Celina, I don't know what you're talking about," Mindy said. "I haven't seen Slade since the last time he came by to pick you up after work."

"Swear?"

"I swear," Mindy said.

Celina deflated. "Oh, good." Her eyes narrowed. "Then why did you look so guilty when I asked about last night?"

"I don't know what you mean," Mindy said, then ducked around her.

"Mindy Catherine MacDougal, you just lied," Celina said.

"No, I didn't," Mindy squawked.

Thankfully, Dr. Fields walked in and interrupted her friend's interrogation. "Ready to begin?"

"Yes." Mindy glanced at Celina and smiled, then rushed off to scrub up.

Two spayings, one neutering, and a paw surgery later, Mindy came out of the back room. Dr. Fields had been kind not to say anything when she dropped three scalpels and handed him the wrong instrument—twice.

Despite vowing to never think about last night again, Mindy couldn't keep her mind off her mystery man. Her thoughts reveled in replaying each moment in vivid color. She could still feel his lips pressed against her neck, and the swirl of his tongue, as he tasted her skin.

Mindy fanned her face and pulled at the collar of her shirt, then walked to the thermostat to check the temperature. It was a balmy seventy-two.

Celina's gaze burned into her. She hadn't said anything more, but it was only a matter of time. Mindy sighed.

"The reason I look so guilty is because I went to Sticks last night," she murmured. "I just wanted to have fun. Feel free for once."

Celina's eyes widened and she came to her feet. "You what!"

"I know you told me that it wasn't my kind of place," she said. "But I had to see for myself." The temp in the room climbed higher.

"What happened?" Celina asked. "Are you hurt? Are you okay?"

"I'm fine." *More or less.* Mindy glanced at her, then looked away. "You were right. It wasn't my kind of place."

"Mindy, what happened?" Celina asked. "What did you

see?”

Huh? “I didn’t see anything other than a lot of good-looking men.” *What is Celina talking about?*

“Just tell me what happened,” she said.

“There was a fight. It was a mess,” Mindy said. “Honestly, I’m embarrassed by the whole situation.”

“You got into a fight?” Celina’s gaze scanned her from head to toe.

“I can’t catch a ball and you think I got into a fight? Seriously?”

“Sorry, I forgot who I was talking to,” Celina said.

She’d confused Mindy with her sister. Celina did that a lot. It was a common mistake and only served to remind her how close this woman and her sister really were.

“Some of the men I met last night got into a fight.” Mindy rubbed her hands over her arms. “I’m fine. Really. A man stepped in and saved me from a bad situation, then I went home.”

“They were fighting over you?” Celina asked.

Mindy’s brow furrowed. “You don’t have to sound so surprised.”

“Sorry. You sure you’re okay?” Celina asked.

She wasn’t, but not for the reason Celina was suggesting. “Positive.”

“Who was he?” Celina asked. “The guy who saved you, I mean.”

Mindy shook her head and sweat trickled down the side of her face. “Don’t know. Didn’t ask.”

Celina frowned in confusion. “What do you mean you didn’t ask?”

Mindy ran a hand through her hair, loosening her ponytail. “It all happened so fast that there wasn’t time,” she said.

Celina’s frown deepened.

Before she could ask another uncomfortable question, the bell on the front door clanged. Mindy’s heart jumped.

It's not the man from last night, she mentally scolded. *It's just a customer.* But that didn't stop her excitement or diminish the swell of hope.

They both walked into the waiting area to see who'd arrived. Celina's boyfriend Slade stood inside the door.

His light gold eyes drifted over Celina and settled on Mindy. He smiled when he saw her, a vibrant, welcoming grin that lit up the room. Mindy smiled back, but couldn't help feeling disappointed.

* * * * *

"Afternoon, ladies." Slade moved deeper into the lobby.

Celina's heart fluttered, but her elation faded when she saw who held his attention. "What are you doing here?"

"I thought I'd see if you want to go to lunch. I have a quick errand to run, but I'll be back in a few," Slade said.

Celina smiled. "Sounds good."

"Mindy," he said. "Have you done something different with your hair?"

Mindy touched the side of her head. "No, it's the same as it's always been."

He studied her appearance. "Hmm, you look different somehow," he said.

Her cheeks flamed.

Celina watched her closely, startled by her friend's response to such an innocent statement. Had she lied about him coming over? Celina shook her head. Mindy had always been a terrible liar. It was how Celina knew her friend had left something out of the story about Sticks. The question was, did it involve her boyfriend?

Slade moved closer.

Celina intercepted him before he could reach Mindy. She slipped her arms around his waist and snuggled next to him.

"You care to join us?" he asked.

Mindy glanced between Celina and Slade. "No, I have to

study, but thanks."

Celina's relief was palpable. "You know Mindy, her nose is always buried in a book. She doesn't have time for socializing. Do you, Mind?"

"Nope," she said, and sounded suddenly sad. "No time."

Slade's amber gaze slid to Celina. "You should try following her example sometime." He kissed her before she could call him out on the insult.

Mindy glared at him, but didn't say anything. "I'll leave you guys to it."

Slade broke the embrace. "Don't bother. I have to run that errand. I'll be back in a few. Be ready," he said to Celina.

"I will." She preened.

Slade walked out of the clinic and headed down the sidewalk. The second he was out of sight, Mindy said, "You shouldn't let him talk to you like that. It's not nice."

Celina glanced at her, but couldn't hold her gaze. "He was kidding."

Mindy stared at her with pity in her eyes. "No, he wasn't," she said. "You deserve better."

Did she? There was a time Celina thought she did, but that was long ago. "I'd worry about your own boyfriend if I were you. Oh, that's right, you don't have one."

Mindy reared back like Celina had slapped her. Hurt followed her initial shock.

Celina rushed forward. "I'm sorry. I didn't mean it." She hugged her.

"It's okay," Mindy said, then pulled out of her embrace. "We're both a little stressed right now."

The phone rang as they walked back into the office. Celina picked it up.

"Breakbend Animal Clinic, may I help you?" she asked. Celina sat as she listened to the person on the other end of the line and took notes.

* * * * *

Mindy was about to check on their patients recovering in the back room when the bell on the front door rang again.

"I'll get it," she said to Celina, and walked back to the lobby.

Mindy stumbled when she caught sight of Marco Faretti. He stood in the doorway with a funny expression on his face. Was he sniffing the air?

"W-what are you doing here?" she asked.

He instantly stopped what he was doing and stepped forward. "It's so good to see you again."

"Slade, you're back fast." Celina came out the door behind Mindy. Her mouth dropped open and her expression changed three times before she managed to pull herself together. "Is this the man who saved you last night?"

Mindy slowly shook her head. What was he doing here? How had he found her? She hadn't told him anything about herself other than she was a student.

"How did you know where I worked?" Mindy asked him.

Marco smiled. The act transformed his handsome face into something truly stunning, but the beautiful mask no longer fooled her. He gave Celina a secretive smile, then said, "I asked around."

"Asked who?" Mindy wanted to know who he'd been questioning. Was it the man from last night? No, it couldn't be him. He didn't know her name.

"Do you want me to get rid of him?" Celina asked. There was hatred in her eyes. Hatred, and...*hurt.*

Mindy shook her head. "No, I'll handle it."

"Almost didn't recognize you, Celina," he said. "You look different with your clothes on."

"Where's your girlfriend, Marco?" Celina asked.

He reddened. "I don't have one. Never did."

Celina flinched.

"I just told you that." He gave her a snide smile. "You

smell...*different*." Marco leaned forward and inhaled deeply. His nose wrinkled and something that looked strangely like fear flashed in his eyes. His smile vanished and he glared at Celina. "What have you gotten yourself into now?"

Celina stammered back. "I don't know what you're talking about. I have work to do." She walked toward the office. Celina hesitated in the doorway. "Leave Mindy alone. She's not like you—or me."

Marco's grin returned. "Run along, Celina. This doesn't concern you."

"I'm standing right here." Mindy scowled at them both.

"If you want, I can phone Slade," Celina said. "He'd have no problem getting rid of him." She glared at Marco.

"Who's Slade?" Marco asked.

Celina lost her bravado. "He's none of your business."

"It's okay," Mindy said. "I got this." She didn't want to make a bad situation worse.

Celina nodded and slipped out of the room.

Mindy turned to Marco. "What are you doing here?"

He glanced at the floor and looked sheepish. "I came to apologize for last night," he said. "My behavior was inexcusable. I'd like to take you to lunch to make up for it."

Mindy wasn't about to go anywhere with him. Not after last night. His sudden appearance only added to her anxiety. She wasn't entirely convinced that he wasn't stalking her.

"I appreciate the apology, but lunch isn't necessary." Mindy recalled the moment Marco punched her mystery man in the face.

Ignoring the hint, Marco grabbed her hand. He ran his fingers gently over her knuckles. "Come on, Mindy. Give a guy a break."

"Like you gave me when you tried to pull me into the woods? Is that the kind of break you're looking for?" Mindy tugged her hand away. His touch didn't feel right, didn't feel like the man who'd held her in his arms last night.

"I said I was sorry. What more do you want me to do?"

Marco asked, then moved in closer, invading her personal space.

"Leave," she said.

"I don't know what Celina has told you about me, but I can guarantee that it was a lie," Marco said. "She and I have a history. We hooked up one time about a month ago. I found out afterwards that she hooks up with a lot of guys, so I cut her loose. It didn't mean anything, I swear."

Mindy bristled. "Didn't mean anything to you? Or to her?" She hoped the shock didn't show on her face. How could he be so callous? After his behavior last night, it shouldn't come as a surprise.

Marco shifted his feet and shoved his hands into his pockets. He glanced past her shoulder toward the door Celina had exited through. "It didn't mean anything to either of us. You can ask her. She'll back me up."

"So that's why you're here," Mindy said. "You think apologizing and asking me to lunch will get you laid."

His amber eyes widened. "No! You have it all wrong. I know you're nothing like her."

"Celina is my best friend. We have a lot in common," Mindy said, though it wasn't true. Celina was Izzy's best friend. They'd become friends by extension. She and Celina were close because of their common love for Izzy, but they had very little in common outside of work.

Marco's expression turned calculating.

"I think you'd better leave." Mindy made her way to the front door, leaving Marco no choice but to follow.

She opened the door and stepped out onto the sidewalk. Marco stopped in front of her.

"I think we got off on the wrong foot," he said.

"No, I'm pretty sure my first impression of you is correct," Mindy said.

* * * * *

Nic was driving along the backside of Main Street, attempting to avoid the tourists in town for a fishing tournament, when he saw the woman from last night come out of a light blue building on his left. His pulse jumped and his palms began to sweat.

She was even more beautiful in the daylight than she'd been under the moonlight. Her light blonde hair was tied back with a red scrunchie and she wore pink scrubs.

The clothes should've looked shapeless, but somehow managed to accentuate her lush curves. Elation quickly turned to confusion when he spotted the pup he'd fought coming out behind her.

The pup grabbed her hand and tried to bring it to his lips. Something dangerous and predatory rose inside Nic. He swerved his truck into the other lane and drove up onto the sidewalk. People scattered to get out of the way.

Nic barely noticed. He was too focused on the woman and the Were standing next to her. He threw the truck into park and jumped out. Nic strode down the sidewalk toward them before he'd formulated what he'd say or do.

The woman was looking at the pup, so she hadn't noticed him yet. She pulled her hand away and told him to leave. It was all the incentive Nic needed. He came up behind the Were and grabbed him by the neck.

"You heard the lady," he said.

The pup swung around. His eyes widened when he saw who had a hold of him. "You again? I thought we settled this last night?" He inhaled. His nostrils flared, and at the same time, his eyes narrowed.

Nic smiled, showing more teeth than was necessary. The pup had picked up the woman's honeyed scent on his skin. "I believe *now* it's settled," he said.

The pup muttered something crude under his breath, then took off down the sidewalk.

Nic watched him go, then turned to the woman. Suddenly alone with her, he was unsure of what to say or do. How do you ask the person you slept with their name without it sounding crass?

She broke the tension building between them by making a weak joke. "Seems like saving me is becoming a habit." She laughed.

Nic rubbed the back of his neck. *Say something. Say anything. Try not to stick your paw in it again.*

"Glad to see that your face is okay." She reached out to touch him, then seemed to think better of it and dropped her arm.

"It was just a scratch." Nic couldn't exactly tell her that he healed almost instantly.

"What are you doing here?" she asked.

"I wasn't following you, if that's what you're thinking," he said, and winced.

Her gaze lowered and she twisted her fingers. "I didn't," she stuttered. "I mean, I wasn't thinking that."

Her pained expression sliced him. Why was he acting like such a jerk? Nic never had trouble speaking to women. Ever!

"I came into town to pick up some parts. I'm a mechanic." He watched to see what her reaction would be to his announcement. He expected her nose to wrinkle or her eyelid to flicker. He expected to see some sign indicating that she preferred suits. She didn't have one, so he continued. "I was driving by and happened to see the pu— guy from last night hassling you."

She glanced up. "I don't know how he found out where I worked," she said. "I didn't tell him."

Nic could tell her exactly how the pup had found her. He'd followed her sweet scent right to the doorstep. The same scent that was filling his lungs and making him dizzy with desire.

"I'm Nic La Croix." He held out his hand. "I don't believe I had a chance to introduce myself last night."

She gave him a small smile. "Me either." She shook his hand. "Mindy MacDougal."

Her touched singed him. Nic's fingers itched to pull her into his arms. He wanted to taste those full lips again. They couldn't possibly be as drugging as he recalled. Before he could act upon the impulse, the door to the clinic flew open and a dark-haired beauty stepped out.

"Is he gone?" She looked up and her breath caught.

Mindy's brow furrowed and she nudged the woman. "Celina, this is Nic. He's the one I told you about earlier."

She'd been talking about him. The thought left Nic unduly pleased, but the feeling faded fast when he thought about what she could've been saying. He hadn't exactly treated her with respect. If anything, he'd behaved just as abominably as the pups. He had to do something. Say something to make the situation right.

Words tangled in his throat, refusing to come out.

"Nice to meet you." Celina eyed him with open curiosity—and undisguised interest.

"You too," Nic said.

Now that he'd taken a better look at her, Nic recognized the dark-haired woman. She was a regular at Sticks. She was also a known groupie who went out of her way to hook up with Weres. Which meant she knew what he was. Apprehension filled him.

Nic didn't think she'd out him in front of Mindy, but he couldn't be sure. His wolf protested inside his head as he made his excuses and left. Nic didn't get far before he turned around and walked back.

He pulled out his wallet. "Here's my number." He handed his business card to Mindy. "I'd be more than happy to take care of that ping in your car for you." He hesitated. "If you want, I could look at it tonight. Won't take long. Just call and leave your address."

Mindy looked at the card, not bothering to hide her stunned expression. "Okay."

Nic nodded and left again. Once more, he stopped short and looked back. "Call me if he comes back."

"I will," she said.

He smiled. "Don't worry, I'll take care of him," Nic said. "I'll make sure he doesn't bother you anymore."

* * * * *

Mindy was too stunned to reply. Her mystery man finally had a name. In her mind, she'd convinced herself that he couldn't possibly look as good as she'd remembered. She'd been wrong. If anything, he was more handsome.

She could get lost in those blue eyes. And no man should have shoulders like that or that tight of a butt.

The moment Nic was out of sight, Celina yanked her around. "I think you left something out of your story," she said. "Want to explain what just happened?"

"I'm not sure," Mindy said. All he'd done was speak to her. Yet her body continued to thrum.

Celina crossed her arms over her chest. "What's going on between you two?"

"Nothing, nothing's going on." The lie slipped from Mindy's lips. How could she explain when she didn't understand?

"Nothing?" Celina snorted. "Honey, that was the definition of something. I could've cut the tension between you two and used it to butter my bread. It was that thick. What do you know about him?"

The warmth on her face had to be coming from the surface of the sun.

"Whoa!" Celina said. "You didn't?" She studied her. "Oh my goodness, you did."

Mindy was pretty sure her heart was going to explode from the sudden rise in her blood pressure.

"I can't believe it," Celina said. "You of all people."

"I told you that I knew how to have a good time. You didn't believe me," Mindy said.

"Oh, honey, is that why you...?" Celina looked in the

direction Nic had gone. "I didn't mean it. I'm such an idiot. Your sister asked me to take care of you."

Mindy snorted. "Izzy asked you to take care of *me*? Out of the two of us, she's the one that needs a keeper."

Celina hugged her. "Please tell me that you didn't sleep with him to prove a point."

Mindy bit her lip. Had that been the only reason? Maybe at first, but it had quickly morphed into something else. Something more incendiary. "That wasn't the only reason." She gave Celina a sly grin.

Her friend laughed. "Well, that's a relief," she said, then sobered. "You need to stay away from Marco. He's bad news. Serious bad news."

"You don't have to convince me of that," Mindy said. "What about Nic?" She held her breath as she waited for Celina's response. If her friend told her that she'd gone out with him, Mindy would be heartbroken, but she'd cut all ties with him.

Celina tilted her head, sending her long brown hair into her face. She absently brushed it back. "I don't really know him," she said. "I've seen him around town and at Sticks a few times, but I don't know anything about him. He keeps to himself." Her gaze fell away.

Mindy's heart slammed against her ribs. What wasn't Celina telling her?

"But?" Mindy asked, because she could clearly hear a "but" coming.

"Just be careful," Celina said. "Nic isn't like other guys."

"What do you mean?" Mindy asked.

Before Celina could respond, the phone inside the clinic rang and she hurried in to answer it.

Saved by the bell.

Mindy looked at the card in her hand. She should throw it away. Forget about last night. Forget all about Nic. That would be the smart thing to do. Too bad her idiot heart had other ideas. She took out her cell phone and punched in the number.

Nic picked up on the first ring.

CHAPTER TEN

Celina could barely hear the woman on the other end of the line over the pounding of her heart. She stayed on the phone only long enough for Mindy to walk into the office and see that she was still on a call. Mindy waved, then continued on into recovery area. The second the door closed; Celina took down the woman's number and disconnected.

Pressure squeezed her lungs until Celina couldn't breathe, while the sour acid of jealousy burned her stomach, leaving her hollow inside. Why Mindy? Why were so many werewolves circling around her friend?

Mindy had never been to Sticks until last night and yet two Weres had already shown up looking for her. She could chalk it up to coincidence, but Marco had all but admitted that he'd tracked Mindy's scent to the front door.

What happened last night? What had Mindy done to garner so much attention? Celina was tempted to ask, so that she could try it next time.

You have Slade, remember? Hopefully there wouldn't be a next time. As the thought filtered through her mind, Celina knew it wasn't true. She could feel him slipping away.

Celina had spent more weekends than she could count at

Sticks. She'd spread her legs for every wolf who'd asked or shown any interest in her. She'd given them exactly what they wanted, in every way they'd wanted it, and her personal sacrifice had gotten her nowhere.

That was until Slade came along.

Bitter jealousy returned. He may claim he had no interest in Mindy, but Celina had seen the look on his face. She'd watched desire shimmer in his amber eyes. He'd had the same hungry look on his face as those other two Weres had when they looked at Mindy.

Tears filled her eyes. *Why her? Why not me?* It wasn't fair.

Mindy was cute and she had curves for days, but Celina was a true beauty. She'd been told so her whole life. Men were attracted to her and she was attracted to men. Bad boys were her fatal weakness.

When Celina had discovered that werewolves existed, she'd been cautiously intrigued. After sleeping with a couple of them, her curiosity morphed into obsession. Werewolves were the ultimate bad boys—thanks to their animal natures, which were never too far from the surface.

They had unbelievable stamina, incredible mouths, and were generous lovers. Best of all, they were overly possessive once they found and claimed their mate.

Celina's preoccupation with Weres had grown so much that being marked by a Were was all she could think about. And now, it looked like Mindy would achieve the goal before she did. The thought seared her insides, leaving her raw with anguish.

She loved Mindy like a sister, but it irritated Celina that she'd been able to garner so much attention without any real effort. The salt in the wound was that Mindy didn't know that werewolves existed.

Why would they be interested in someone so clueless? They were never quick to expose their secrets, but they had to know they'd have to eventually if they continued to pursue her. Unless of course they were just after sex.

Sex she could live with. It was an emotional attachment that would be unbearable.

Cold settled around Celina's heart. Maybe it was time she told Mindy that her sister wasn't crazy. That the monsters Izzy warned her about were real. If she did that, Celina wouldn't have to worry about losing Slade or the other wolves coming around. Mindy wouldn't want anything to do with any of them.

CHAPTER ELEVEN

Mindy made a quick trip to the grocery store after work before rushing home to get ready for Nic's arrival. She fed all her animals and talked to each one about their day, then put the cooked roast and potatoes she'd picked up into the oven to warm.

She threw together a salad and set the bowl inside the refrigerator. Mindy didn't know if Nic would want to stay for dinner, but she wanted to be ready just in case. She walked into her bedroom and found a dead mouse on her pillow.

"Hannibal!"

Her one-eyed orange tabby came strolling into the room. He rubbed against her leg, arching his back and purring with pride. Mindy rolled her eyes and scratched him behind the ears.

"You have to stop bringing me presents, or in your case, displaying your kills." She stroked him again, then picked up her pillow and carried it to the back door.

Mindy unlocked the door and tossed the dead mouse outside, then stripped the pillowcase off and threw it in the laundry hamper. She retrieved a clean pillowcase from the dresser drawer in Izzy's old bedroom and grabbed one of her sister's sweaters while she was at it.

With the clean pillowcase in place, she walked into the bathroom and turned the shower on. Mindy had just tugged on the end of her shirt when she heard scratching at the back door.

Hannibal was perched on her bed. Had Tart somehow gotten out when she removed the mouse? God, she hoped not. She did not need a litter of puppies.

Mindy dropped her shirt and walked down the hall. She moved the curtain aside and gasped. What was he doing here? She turned the lock and opened the door. The wolf-hybrid she and Celina had rescued stared at her with startling amber eyes. At first she was scared, then he whimpered.

"How did you get here, big boy?" Mindy slowly stepped out onto her small back porch and looked around. She didn't want to startle him. "Celina was supposed to have taken you to the preserve."

They'd decided that he wasn't someone's pet, but he also wasn't entirely wild. He'd obviously been around people at some point, but given his size it would be better if he had somewhere safe to roam.

He nudged her hand with his massive head.

Mindy's fingers sank into his thick fur. "Are you hungry?"

His tail wagged.

"Well, come on in. Let's get you something to eat."

Tart, her rescue poodle, came running out of the living room straight at them. Mindy had completely forgotten that she was loose.

She tried to cut her off, but the large, three-legged poodle was in heat and easily snaked around her. She immediately whimpered and spun around to entice the big male. If the hybrid mounted her, there was no way Mindy would get them apart without losing a hand.

The wolf-hybrid sniffed Tart's bottom and growled. The

sound sent chills across Mindy's skin. Not the reaction she expected from a male canine, especially one who was part wolf. Tart yelped and scampered away. He watched her go, but made no move to follow.

"You are an odd duck, my friend," Mindy said. She'd never seen a male dog of any kind turn away a bitch in heat. "Let's get you some food."

His massive paws were silent as he trailed her to the kitchen.

"Sit," she said, then grabbed a plate out of the cupboard. Mindy pulled the roast out of the oven.

The hybrid shoved his nose between her legs and sniffed, then licked her jeans.

Mindy almost dropped the roast on his head. She quickly set the pot on the counter and grabbed his nose to move it away. "Watch it there, big guy."

She sliced a generous hunk off the roast and put it on the plate. The meat hadn't been in the oven long, so it wasn't too hot.

"Easy," she said, then lowered the plate to the floor. "While you finish that, I'm going to call Celina and find out what happened."

The hybrid gobbled his food down, then wandered back the way he'd came in. He sat next to the back door and whimpered to be let out.

"You're not going anywhere," Mindy said. "So get comfortable." She kept an eye on Tart to make sure she didn't try to entice the hybrid again.

Mindy punched in Celina's number. It went straight to voicemail. She was probably sucking face with Slade. She waited for the beep.

"Celina, call me when you get this message. I have the hybrid here with me. We need to talk." She disconnected the call and set the cell phone on the counter. The house was quiet—too quiet. She looked around.

Tart huddled in the corner next to the couch, trembling.

There was a small puddle of urine beneath her.

"Terrific," Mindy muttered.

She poked her head in the hall to see what the hybrid was up to. A gentle breeze brushed her face. The back door was wide open and the hybrid was gone.

"How did you..." Mindy raced down the hall and ran out into the yard. She scanned the tree line, but there was no sign of him.

Mindy walked back into the house and stopped to examine the door. The glass and the frame appeared to be intact. Everything looked perfectly normal. Maybe she'd forgotten to close it properly and it had blown open? It was the only explanation that made any sense. It was either that or the hybrid had figured out how to turn a knob.

Her gaze swept the yard one final time, then she closed the door and locked it. Mindy didn't have time to go looking for him in the woods. Nic would be here any minute.

Mindy took a quick shower and put some makeup on, then slipped Izzy's sweater over her head. She tried on three pairs of jeans, giving each one the butt check in the mirror. None of them passed. She grabbed a pair of Izzy's and pulled them on. She should've known they'd be perfect.

She'd just tugged her shoes on when the doorbell rang. Mindy took a deep breath and glanced one last time in the mirror to check her appearance. It shouldn't have been so important, but she wanted to look nice for Nic.

"You look fine," she muttered, then wandered into the living room.

Nic was early.

Eagerness is a good sign. Isn't it?

Mindy planted a smile on her face and pulled the door open. Her grin faded as she came face to face with Marco Faretti. Startled, she stepped back. Shock quickly turned to fear.

"What are you doing here, Marco?" She glanced up the road, hoping to spot Nic's truck in the distance.

"I came here to finish our conversation without being interrupted," he said.

Mindy's knuckles whitened from holding the door so tight. "Now's not a good time."

Marco's gaze started at her head and slowly worked its way down before reversing direction. "You going out? If you're heading to Sticks, maybe I'll see you there? We never did finish that drink."

Mindy shook her head. "I'm not going out," she said. "And I'm definitely not going back to that bar."

As was his habit, he crowded her with his body. "Why not? I thought you had a good time."

Scared, Mindy held her ground. "I think we remember last night differently," she said. "You need to go. I don't appreciate being stalked and I'm expecting company any minute."

Marco's amber eyes narrowed. "Is it that wolf from the Fortier estate?"

Wolf? Was that some kind of slang for a male slut? Mindy didn't keep up with modern slang, so she wasn't sure.

"I assume you're talking about Nic," she said.

"Is that his name?" His lip curled in disgust. Before she could respond, he continued, "I guess you are like your friend Celina after all. You know where to find me once he kicks you to the curb." Marco dropped down a step and his nose wrinkled. "Is Celina here?"

"No. Why?"

"Thought I smelled her," he said.

Mindy inhaled, but didn't smell anything other than the roast. "I don't know what you're talking about."

Marco poked his head in the door and dragged air into his lungs.

"What are you doing? I told you she wasn't here," she said. "You need to leave. Now!"

He scowled at her and walked to his car. He changed direction at the last second and slipped behind her house.

Fear pulsed inside of her. What was he doing?

"I mean it, Marco," she shouted. "If you don't leave this second, I'm calling the police!"

At first, Mindy didn't think that he'd heard her, then she saw him sprint across the yard. His face was pale and his wide amber eyes kept scanning the tree line. It was a relief to see that he was taking her threat seriously.

Marco didn't stop watching the woods until he was behind the wheel. Gravel flew as he tore out of her driveway.

Mindy watched him leave. It wasn't until he was out of sight that she was finally able to let go of the front door.

* * * * *

Nic passed the pup on the road. There was only one place he could be coming from. Fear demolished his nervousness. He needed to get to Mindy. Make sure she was okay. He stomped down hard on the gas. Nic's truck roared as he raced down the road.

He found the address and hurried into the driveway. Nic threw his truck into park and jumped out, not bothering to turn it off. He leapt up her front stairs and pounded on the door.

"Marco, I told you to leave," Mindy shouted.

"It's not Marco," Nic rumbled.

"Nic?" Mindy opened the door. Her pale face and trembling hands said all he needed to know. "Sorry, I thought you were someone else."

"Are you okay?" he asked.

Nic didn't wait for her to answer. He simply pulled her into his arms and ran his hands over her body. He needed to see for himself that she was unharmed. What was the pup doing here? How had he found out where she lived?

She allowed him to comfort her for a minute, then Mindy slowly moved away. The awkwardness that had been there earlier in the day returned.

Nic cleared his throat. "I'll need the keys to your car. You still want me to take a look at it, right?"

"Yes, of course." Mindy lifted the keys off the hook beside the door. "Here." She handed the key ring to him.

"It won't take long," he said.

"Take your time," Mindy said. "I was just finishing up the side dishes for dinner. Would you like to stay? I made enough for two."

She was okay. He'd seen so with his own eyes. He should fix her car and leave, but Nic didn't want to go. He wanted to spend more time with her.

"Sure," he said.

"Great." She smiled, and his stomach fluttered.

Nic walked back to his truck. He could feel Mindy's eyes on him. Everywhere she looked, a wave of heat followed. He flexed his hands and turned off his engine before grabbing his toolbox. Twenty minutes later, he'd finished the minor adjustment to get rid of the pinging and had her car humming once more.

He dropped the hood and was walking back to his truck to put his toolbox inside when he caught a strange scent wafting on the air. Nic placed the toolbox on the seat and slowly shut the door. He raised his head and carefully smelled the area around him.

What was that?

Nic had never smelled anything like it. He stepped away from his truck and walked into the yard. The scent grew fainter. Nic frowned and switched direction. The breeze brought the odor again. This time stronger. He scanned the trees. Nothing moved. The hair on Nic's neck rose and the wolf inside him surfaced.

The door opened. "Are you done?" Mindy asked.

Nic nodded, but continued to stare at the woods.

"What is it?" Mindy stepped out of the house onto the porch.

"It's nothing," Nic said.

"Marco isn't back. Is he?" Her voice quivered.

Nic turned away from the woods. "No." He shook his head. "He's not around. You don't have to worry."

The relief on her beautiful face was palpable. "Good," she said. "I just wanted to let you know that dinner is ready."

"I'll be right in," Nic said. "Just need to get something out of my truck."

Mindy nodded and walked back into the house.

Nic waited until she was inside, then scented the woods once more. The odd odor was gone, but its absence didn't alleviate his unease. If anything, it made it worse.

As part of the Moonlight Kin, there weren't many scents he couldn't identify. He rubbed the back of his neck and walked to the house. The fact that he couldn't place this one worried him.

Chapter Twelve

The second he stepped through the door into the living room, chaos erupted. Squawks, hisses, and barks collided in a glass-shattering cacophony. Nic was immediately hit with sensory overload.

Mindy's ranch-style house was neat and clean. Nic doubted a human would detect the various scents, but to a Were it was like taking a stroll through a zoo after a sinus rinse. So many scents. Too many. Including an unusual one that escaped him.

He held his hands over his sensitive ears and his eyes watered as he slowly looked around. Various types of animals were scattered throughout the cozy living room.

"Hush!" Mindy said. "What's wrong with you guys? Behave, we have company." She turned to Nic. "I'm sorry. They don't normally act like this. Have a seat while I check on dinner." She pointed to the rose-colored couch under the window.

Nic wasn't surprised by the uproar. A predator was in their midst and they didn't like it one bit. Between the scents and the noise, Nic couldn't hear himself think. The animals were making him edgy.

Still, he found himself sitting down. Nic told himself it was to be polite, but he was only lying to himself.

"Can I get you a drink?" She walked into what he presumed was the kitchen.

"I could use a beer." It was an understatement.

A one-eyed cat took one sniff of him and hissed. Its orange fur rose on its back and its tail straightened as it prepared to attack.

Nic bared his teeth and growled low in his chest. The cat snarled and ran into the corner under a side table.

Mindy's three-legged poodle showed no fear at all when it approached. It licked his jeans and whirled around to show him its butt, then proceeded to hump his leg. Nic tried to shake the dog off, but it was determined to entice him, since it was in heat. He groaned. This was a nightmare.

There was another loud squawk. Nic flinched and looked over at the cage hanging from a chain attached to the ceiling. A gray parrot cocked its head to look at him, then said, "Nice doggy." The comment was followed by a string of expletives that would shame a fleet of intoxicated sailors.

Movement in the corner of his eye drew his gaze away from the foul-mouthed feathered menace. A green, tailless lizard marched across the couch toward him. When it got close, it did a strange rocking dance that Nic was sure was meant to intimidate him.

He had to leave. This was too much. Nic shook the randy poodle off his leg and stood. Mindy came into the room as he was about to make his way to the front door. She was carrying two beers.

"Where are you going?" she asked.

He didn't want to hurt her feelings, but he had to go. "What is all this?" The question surprised them both.

Mindy set the beers on the coffee table, then walked over to pick up the cat cowering in the corner. "They're strays." She stroked the feline. "This is Hannibal. I named him that because he constantly kills things and presents the bodies to me." She pointed to the poodle. "That's Tart. She humps anything that moves."

"Go to your kennel." She herded the dog into a back room and shut the door, then walked back into the living room. "Now that her wounds are healed, I plan to get her fixed. Her owners abused her. It took me two months just to get her to the point where I could pet her without her flinching."

Nic looked at the parrot, who continued his foul-mouthed tirade.

"That's Perry. I'm pretty sure he has Tourette's syndrome," Mindy said.

It took Nic a second to register what she'd said. When he did, he threw his head back and laughed. "Tourette's?"

Mindy had the grace to look embarrassed. "It's not out of the realm of possibility. Animals tend to have a lot of the same issues that humans have. They have feelings. They dream. They have worth, though a lot of people don't believe so."

The flutter in Nic's chest turned into a full-on drumbeat. He rubbed the spot and wished more than anything that Mindy wasn't human. Her heart obviously held a lot of love for her menagerie. He could see it in the way she looked at them, the way she spoke about them. No doubt her capacity to love would extend to any relationship she had.

Longing, deep and fierce tugged at him. He had to get away from this line of thinking. It would only end in heartache and disappointment. He glanced at the lizard. "What about him? What's his story?"

Mindy scratched Hannibal under the chin. "That's George. He had an unfortunate accident that involved Hannibal." The cat purred at the mention of its name. "But they're friends now. Mostly."

"Are you keeping them for any particular reason?" he asked. It was normal for humans to have pets, but this was more than that.

Mindy frowned. "I don't understand the question."

"Why are they here?" he asked.

"Because they had nowhere else to go, and with Isabel gone there's even more room for them to roam," she said.

Of course she did. Nic sank back down on the couch. "Who's Isabel?" She was probably the animal scent he couldn't place.

Mindy handed him a beer, then sat in the chair across from him. Hannibal settled on her lap, but Nic noticed the cat didn't take its good eye off him.

"My sister."

"I'm sorry. Is she dead?" he asked as delicately as he could. He didn't want to dredge up painful memories.

Mindy laughed. "No, she's just-" she paused as she searched for the right word, "-eccentric. She ran off to New Orleans a few weeks ago to find herself." Mindy rolled her eyes. "Or something like that."

"Ah." Nic could tell there was more to the story, but he didn't press. "So how did this all start?"

"As you know, I work at the animal clinic in Breakbend," she said. "I'm also a full-time student at Clarkston Greenburg University. I'll finish at the end of this year." Mindy took a sip of her beer.

"What's your major?" he asked.

"Veterinary medicine. I prefer to work with animals. People can be confusing," she said, then sucked in her cheeks, as if doing so would draw the admission back inside her mouth.

Her ambition was admirable and her love of strays enduring. Thus far, the only *flaw* he'd found was her humanity.

"I'm surprised you found time to go out to the bar with that kind of schedule," he said.

Mindy brushed her shoulder-length hair back and suddenly looked uncomfortable. "I normally don't. Anytime I have free time, it's spent studying."

Nic couldn't smell her wonderful scent over her collection of critters, so he couldn't tell if she'd lied. "What brought you to Sticks?" he asked, though he wasn't sure he wanted to know the answer.

What if she knows what he is? What if the innocent act is just that—an act?

Mindy's brown gaze slipped away and she stopped petting the cat. "About the other night...I should apologize. I'm not normally like that. I'm sorry if I—" She paused. "Gave you the wrong impression."

Good to know, Nic thought. His relief was palpable, but she still hadn't answered his question. "Have you ever been to the bar before?"

Pink blossomed in her cheeks and spread down her neck. "No," she said. "A good friend told me about it."

Nic's brow rose. "Some friend," he chided, his voice harsher than he'd intended.

Mindy's eyes widened in alarm, then her gaze locked on him. "It's not like that. Celina is a good friend. She warned me not to go."

"But you went anyway?" He made it a question.

Mindy stiffened in her seat. "I'm twenty-five. I'm old enough to make my own decisions."

Nic held up his hands. "Darlin', you'll get no argument from me." Images of their carnal encounter flashed through his mind. Nic's body responded in an instant. He put his beer down and shot to his feet. "I forgot to check something in your car." Self-preservation drove him to the door.

"I'll set the table while you do that." Her voice petered out and she looked embarrassed.

"Sounds good," he said. "I'll be right back." Nic stepped outside. He hated that he'd made Mindy feel uncomfortable in her own home. It seemed like every time he opened his mouth, stupid came out.

He mentally cursed, then strode across the lawn toward her car. Nic fiddled around with the wires for ten minutes.

Long enough for him to pull himself together, then he slowly walked back to the house.

Mindy wasn't in the living room and neither was her cat. She'd covered Perry's cage with a sheet, which quieted him down. George sat in an aquarium tucked in the corner that Nic hadn't noticed when he'd first come into her home.

"I'm in here," she said. "Did you fix it?"

"Fix what?" Nic asked, forgetting that he was supposed to be out checking something on her car. The house smelled like beef, along with the alluring scent of Mindy. He followed the sound of her voice into a small room off her kitchen.

Candles flickered on the table between two blue placemats. She'd positioned a roast at one end and potatoes and a salad at the other. His beer was sitting next to the roast.

"Take a seat," she said. "I hope you're not a vegetarian."

The thought made him smile. She had no idea what a carnivore he could be. "Smells good."

* * * * *

Mindy's hands shook as she passed the knife to Nic. "You want to do the honors?" She hated that she was so nervous.

He didn't hesitate. Nic took the butcher knife and quickly carved the roast. He lifted a couple of slices and placed them on her plate.

"Thank you," she said.

Mindy was still having a hard time believing that he was really in her house. She hadn't expected to ever see him again, but she was grateful that she did. It proved that she hadn't been wrong about their connection. There *was* something simmering between them. Something elusive, but tangible nonetheless.

Nic served himself, then waited for her to pass the vegetables. He didn't take many. The roast covered much of his plate.

"Can we start over?" she asked. "I know that's kind of a weird request, considering everything that's transpired, but I'd really like to begin again."

Nic looked up from his food and smiled. "I'd like that, too."

Mindy grinned. "My name is Mindy MacDougal." She held out her hand.

He took it gently. "Nic La Croix." Heat simmered in his blue eyes, leaving her breathless.

"So, Nic," she said, "tell me about yourself."

Some of the heat faded and his expression became guarded.

Unease settled into Mindy's stomach. "You aren't married, are you?"

Nic shook his head, sending his shaggy, light brown hair bouncing. "No. I wouldn't have... What I mean to say is, I wouldn't have been at the bar alone if I were attached in any way. What about you?" he asked. "Do you have anyone special in your life?"

Mindy played with her fork. "No, not for a while now. There really hasn't been time. What with school and all." *And looking after Izzy.* She placed her fork on the plate and picked up her beer. Mindy took a sip. The drink burned down her throat. "So are you from around here?"

"No," he said. "But I've been here for the past eleven years."

"Almost makes you a local," she said.

His eyes crinkled when he laughed.

Mindy loved the sound. It was deep, throaty, and infectious. From the creases next to his eyes, Nic looked like he laughed a lot. It made her want to say something funny just so she could hear him laugh again.

"You said you were a mechanic," she added.

Nic nodded. "I work on the Fortier estate. They have a big garage there." He watched her closely when he said the name.

Mindy wasn't sure what he was looking for, but he must've been satisfied with what he saw because he seemed to relax. "I'm aware of the place, but only because I think Celina mentioned it before. You said Fortier, right?" she asked.

"Yes," Nic said.

"Is the family any relation to the software mogul?"

"One and the same," he said.

"Ah, good for you," she said. "Thought the name sounded vaguely familiar. I don't really keep up with high-society news."

Nic took a deep swallow of his beer. "Has Celina ever been out to the estate?"

Mindy shrugged. "I don't think so, but I honestly wouldn't know."

"I thought you said she was your friend," Nic said.

Mindy's stomach tightened. "She is, but we don't do everything together. She's actually Izzy's best friend. We've always hung out together, but it's only recently that we've grown close."

"I understand," he said.

Did he? Did he really?

"Listen, about the other night." Mindy hated to bring the subject up again, but she thought it was necessary to clear the air.

Nic held up his hand. "Mindy, you don't have to explain," he said. "I don't normally do that kind of thing either."

She exhaled loudly, then laughed. "I guess we both were swept up in the moment."

"That's putting it mildly," he muttered. "I definitely got carried away." This time his blue eyes sparkled.

Memories of his rough hands gliding over her skin, his firm lips devouring hers, flittered through her mind. Mindy picked up her napkin and dabbed at the gathering moisture on her forehead.

"So," she said. "Have you always been a mechanic?"

"No, but I've always enjoyed tinkering on anything with a motor in it. Fixing cars began as a hobby and quickly became a profession," he said. "Does that bother you?"

Why would his vocation bother her? Mindy was genuinely confused by the question. "No, should it?"

Nic shrugged and put his fork down. "You just struck me as the kind of woman who prefers suits."

Her brow furrowed. "That's only because you don't know me very well." Did he really think she was so shallow? She looked at him. Maybe he did.

Mindy hadn't meant to give Nic that impression. Of course, it was hard to make a good impression, when you were flat on your back, half naked, sprawled across the bed of a pick-up truck.

He fidgeted in his seat. "I didn't mean anything by it. It was just an observation," Nic said.

"Well, you're wrong," Mindy said. "I've had to work for everything I've achieved." She'd had no choice, since Izzy's antics had bankrupted their parents. "I'm not interested in social climbing. I want to be a vet because I love animals, not because I have dreams of marrying a fellow doctor."

"Got it," he said.

They continued making small talk throughout the rest of the dinner. Despite the rough start, Mindy found herself truly enjoying Nic's company. When the meal was done, he helped her clear the table and wash the dishes.

After they were dried and put away, Nic said, "I'd better head out. Thank you for the lovely meal."

"Thanks for fixing my car," Mindy said.

"It was the least I could do," he said.

He didn't owe her anything, but Mindy didn't want him to leave yet. "I picked up dessert." She opened the refrigerator and pulled out a chocolate cake.

Nic paled. "Sorry, I'm allergic to chocolate, but thank

you."

Mindy was all out of excuses to keep him there, so she walked him to the front door.

Chapter Thirteen

Nic's gaze roamed over her face. This was it. Once he walked out that door, they probably wouldn't see each other again. It was the right thing to do. They were two different species. All that was left was to step out onto the porch.

He stared at Mindy. Throughout the whole meal, all he could think about was kissing her. His eyes locked onto her lips. They were full, rosy and just begging to be explored.

Nic slowly touched her hand and threaded his fingers through hers. He brought her knuckles to his mouth and pressed a chaste kiss to the back of them. He watched Mindy's breath catch and her pulse jump beneath her skin.

He tugged her hand, bringing her closer to him. "I want to kiss you," he murmured. "But I'm afraid if I do, I won't want to stop."

Mindy moistened her lips.

Nic groaned and closed his eyes. "Do you have any idea how beautiful you are? How *tempting*?" he asked. "I can hardly keep my hands off you. I should leave. It wasn't my intention to come over here and seduce you again. I really did want to make up for my bad behavior last night." He released her and turned to make good on his word.

Mindy caught his arm. "Don't go."

Nic almost didn't hear her above the blood raging in his veins. "I need you to be sure." It was a plea and a prayer.

"I'm sure," she whispered.

"Why you?" He leaned his forehead against hers.

Mindy laughed. "I've been asking myself the same question since last night."

Nic slipped his hand around her neck and slowly lowered his head, giving her plenty of time to move away—to escape him.

She didn't. Instead, Mindy's lips parted in welcome.

Nic seized her mouth, capturing her in a fierce kiss. The taste of her melted across his tongue. She was pure ambrosia. He followed the tantalizing flavor, exploring her depths thoroughly, wanting more. The room spun as he deepened the embrace.

Mindy's fingers fluttered over his chest, coming to rest above his pounding heart.

Nic's body hardened and his hands fisted in her shirt, bunching the sweater's material. Her skin heated. With the rise in temperature came the delicious, musky aroma of hot moist woman.

He broke the embrace, his ragged breath ripped from his chest. "Tell me to leave now and I might be able to go," he rasped. It was a last-ditch effort to save himself. To save her innocence from his dark world. "I'm not strong enough to walk away on my own." The confession scorched his soul.

Mindy's brown eyes dilated. She couldn't seem to catch her breath. She pressed her swollen lips together and swallowed hard.

"Please don't go," she murmured.

"I don't want us to regret this, this time," he said.

Her long lashes fluttered to conceal her eyes. "I don't regret the last time." She ran a hand over her arm and bit her lip. "Do you?"

Nic's denial was swift and fierce. "Hell no!"

* * * * *

If she told him to leave this second, Nic would. His stern expression said his offer was real. If that happened, there was a very good chance she wouldn't see him again. Panic hit, squeezing her throat. That was the last thing Mindy wanted.

Still, she didn't know much about this man. Was she really going to invite him into her bed?

He saved you from Marco twice. He fixed your car. He let Tart hump his leg. And he didn't run away.

That said a lot about his character. She stared into his dark blue eyes, watching the waves of passion wash over them. She could get lost in those eyes. It wouldn't take much to be swept away. Mindy was already halfway there.

"I don't want to be alone tonight," she said. "I'm tired of feeling lonely." This time it wasn't her wild side talking. This time it was the *real* Mindy baring her soul.

Nic shuddered as her words struck their mark.

"Me too." Nic cradled her face between his large hands and slowly tilted her head to capture her lips once more.

The kiss was so devastatingly tender that it brought tears to Mindy's eyes. With that one kiss, Nic conveyed all the emotions he kept bottled inside. Mindy tasted his fear, his need, his compassion, and his loneliness.

She also discovered a deeper, darker, wilder undercurrent. The last should've scared her, but instead she was drawn to it, drawn to him. Mindy savored every one of his emotions, grateful that he'd been willing to leave himself so utterly exposed.

He walked her backwards toward the hall, never breaking the kiss. Nic reached for the first doorknob he came to. Mindy stopped him before he could open the door.

"That's Izzy's room," she murmured against his lips.

Mindy grabbed his shirt and kept moving, taking him

farther down the hall. The second door they encountered was cracked.

* * * * *

Nic pushed it open. A neat bedroom came into view. The only thing he cared about at the moment was the queen-sized bed with the rose-colored comforter and pillows piled high. The room smelled like Mindy. He flicked the light on and guided her inside, then kicked the door closed with his foot. As soon as he heard it click shut, Nic stripped her clothes off.

The sweater went first. It was followed by her jeans. By the time he finished, all Mindy had on was her lacy white bra and matching panties. She toed her shoes off, then stepped out of her pants.

Nic ran his fingertips over the swell of her breasts and watched her nipples tighten beneath the material. "I didn't get to see these last night." He slipped one finger under the strap and slowly slid it off her shoulder. "I dreamed about them. About you."

Gooseflesh rose on her arms.

"Cold?" he asked, knowing she wasn't.

Mindy shook her head. "Hot," she said. "If I get any warmer, I will be scalding."

"Then I hope you like the heat, darlin', because you're about to get a lot hotter." It was a vow Nic intended to keep.

He cupped her fullness, feeling the heavy weight of her in his hands. He brushed his thumbs over the front of her swollen flesh, loving the sound of her breath as it caught in her throat.

His lips found hers once more and he reached behind her. With a flick of his wrist, her bra gaped open and fell to the floor. Nic broke the kiss to look at her.

"Oh, have mercy," he said, then ran his tongue over the soft swell before capturing her nipple between his teeth.

Mindy gasped and clutched his head. Nic feasted on her flesh, turning it bright red. She was even sweeter tasting here. He latched on to the other nipple, making sure to give it equal attention. Mindy swelled before his eyes, ripening like a summer berry.

Nic sucked and nibbled until her knees threatened to give out, then he coaxed her onto the bed. Her blonde hair spread across the rose comforter, haloing her head. "I didn't get to explore you the way that I wanted to. I intend to make up for that oversight right now."

He grabbed Mindy by her ankles and pulled her forward until her bottom rested at the edge of the bed. He grabbed her panties and yanked them off, then dropped to his knees and inhaled. His head spun as her delicious aroma ensnared him.

Drool threatened to drip from his mouth as he carefully parted her legs to reveal her hidden cleft. She blossomed before him. His incisors lengthened and his eyes glowed. Nic's gaze dropped to keep her from seeing the effect she had on him. *On his wolf.*

Nic settled his wide shoulders between her thighs and slowly took his first real taste of her. Spice and honey exploded on his tongue. Nic's body instantly hardened to the point of pain. He dipped in again and her juices ran down his chin.

Nic wanted to bury himself inside her, experience the warm, tight embrace he'd felt the other night. But he wouldn't. Not yet. He wasn't finished tasting her, feasting on her yet. He wanted to sup on Mindy's flesh, devour her sex until all that remained was a deeply sated woman.

Nic stopped his gentle exploration and dove in with gusto. He licked, stroked, and worried her flesh with his teeth until she plumped beneath his firm lips.

Mindy's knees locked around his head and her thighs quivered. She tried to squirm up the bed when the sensations got to be too much, but Nic wasn't having it. He held on to her hips and slid his hands beneath bottom, tilting her to give him better access, then continued to feast.

* * * * *

She couldn't think. Couldn't breathe. Her entire world was centered on his amazing mouth and what it was doing to her. Pressure built inside her. A pressure the likes of which she'd never experienced before. Her hands clenched the duvet as she tried to hold on to her world, as it rotated faster.

Nic swirled his tongue around and around her until lights flashed behind her eyelids. Mindy's body bucked and she pressed her lips together hard to keep from screaming. She tasted blood and didn't care.

He sucked her between his teeth and bit down. The flare of pain amidst all the pleasure sent her spiraling over the edge, as the mother of all orgasms roared through her, engulfing her in flames. This time Mindy did scream Nic's name.

* * * * *

Mindy's cries rang in his ears as she rippled around his tongue. Nic couldn't stop the smile from spreading across his face. Mindy's legs dropped open and her body liquefied. She was everything he'd remembered and more.

Nic grabbed his shirt off the floor and wiped his mouth, then slowly climbed to his feet. He stared down at her. Mindy's pale flesh had turned a delectable shade of pink. Her nipples jutted toward the ceiling, all but begging to be nibbled on again. He watched her body quake. Nic would remember this moment for the rest of his life.

He repositioned her until she was further onto the bed, then Nic settled on top of her. He kissed Mindy tenderly and brushed the damp hair away from her face.

"You aren't finished yet. Are you?" he asked.

Mindy licked her lip and tried to speak. After a minute she gave up and shook her head.

"Good," he said. "Because I'm just getting started."

This time Nic didn't sheathe himself. He wanted to know what—if anything—would happen when they had sex skin to skin. He didn't expect a repeat of the other night. With his wolf firmly leashed, Nic didn't feel as out of control.

"I don't have any diseases," he said, kissing her again. "Are you on birth control?"

Mindy nodded.

"I know I'm asking you to trust me with your life, but I swear to you that I'd never do anything to put you in harm's way."

She stared at him for so long he thought she was going to reject him, then finally she answered. "Okay, but if you're lying, I will cut you up into little pieces and feed you to Hannibal."

"I'm not. Thank you for your trust." The words had barely left his mouth, when Nic surged forward burying himself inside her molten core. The sensation shocked his system, leaving him winded.

It was the first time he'd *ever* gone bareback in woman. That he'd done so with a human wasn't lost on him. It was...it was...*incredible*.

Nic held himself still and tried to catch his breath. Mindy's legs rose and she wrapped her knees around him, holding him close. Her level of trust made his heart soar. It also terrified him.

So far, so good. No odd reactions. No internal swelling.

For some reason, the thought that the whole thing might've been because of the full moon left him oddly disappointed.

You should be elated. This is what you wanted.

Nic rolled his hips and thrust forward, feeling her velvet muscles grip him. Fire burned down his spine and he had to fight the urge to rut like a beast inside her.

He found Mindy's mouth and continued his carnal invasion while he glided forward, embedding himself to the hilt. Nic shuddered. She was perfect. Everything about her seemed to fit. He pulled out until only the tip of him remained inside her.

Mindy whimpered and pushed down upon him, seeking more.

Nic's lips slid over her jaw as he easily slipped in and out of her fiery sheath. "I didn't think it would be possible, but it's even better tonight."

He concentrated on keeping a steady rhythm, so he could build the tension inside of her. He wanted to hear her scream his name again. Mindy tightened around him. Nic found her earlobe and sucked on it, feeling her core pulse in response.

He sucked harder until Mindy writhed beneath him and rocked her hips to meet him thrust for thrust. Her choppy breathing told him she wouldn't last much longer.

Nic hooked his elbows under her knees and lifted her legs higher. The position allowed him to go deeper. Mindy mewed, and her head thrashed from side to side as he pounded into her.

"I can't. I can't," she gasped. In the next breath, she convulsed, her body doing its best to milk him dry.

Nic kissed the side of her neck and felt a deep, primitive tug. His tongue swirled over the spot where her neck met her shoulder. While Mindy was coming apart in his arms, Nic was being pulled under by something far stronger.

He continued to surge into her as she thrashed beneath him. Nic nibbled on her neck, then sucked on her skin. Mindy's entire body stiffened and she let out a keening cry as a second release hit close on the heels of the first.

Nic's world narrowed. All he could see was her pulse fluttering in her neck. He rolled his hips and nudged her cervix. The second it kissed her center, he swelled. The change swept over his body. Nic couldn't stop it. In truth, he didn't want to.

"I'm sorry, but I can't resist," he murmured, then bit down on Mindy's neck.

Blood poured into his mouth. Nic swallowed it, greedily lapping her up, taking her essence into him. He was careful not to lose a drop.

Mindy whimpered and tried to pull away.

His growl stopped her. It was far too late to escape. His wolf had her now. It was determined to mark her, *inside and out*. But first it demanded her submission.

Mindy's body tensed.

Nic tightened his grip on her neck. A few seconds passed, then she stroked his head and relaxed beneath him. His wolf howled in triumph as Nic took more of her blood.

Instinct told him when he'd had enough. Nic stopped drinking and licked the tender bite until the blood quit flowing. Mindy was going to have one hell of a hickey, but it couldn't be helped.

Nic wanted her to taste him—to complete the mating ritual—but he knew she wasn't ready. His ragged breathing finally returned to normal, but his hips continued to flex as he spilled his seed inside her. Nic kissed her neck and nuzzled her cheek.

* * * * *

"Sorry, I lost control again. Being inside you makes me crazy with desire," he said.

Mindy touched his shadowed cheek. "I feel the same way," she whispered. "You make me want things I've never thought about. It's like a part of you is inside of me."

He glanced down and grinned.

Her heart flip-flopped. "You know what I mean."

"Yeah, I know." He rubbed his nose against hers.

"I guess this means we'll have to figure all this out together," she said.

"It won't be easy," he said.

Nic was still hard and heavy inside of her. She'd never known a man could have such endurance. That hadn't been her experience in the past. Of course Mindy only had her ex to compare him to, and it wasn't a fair comparison.

"We seem to end up naked every time we get together," she said.

He kissed her throat. "There are worse ways to end up. Take my word for it."

Mindy shoved at his chest.

Nic laughed and sat up, taking her with him since their bodies were still connected.

"I think you've ruined me for other men," Mindy joked, though it was the truth.

Something dark crossed Nic's handsome features and his eyes glittered. "It might be best if you avoid other men for a while."

Mindy arched a brow. "Is that so?"

His smile returned in a flash, but it didn't reach his eyes. "We need time to get to know one another. Can't really do that properly if you're seeing other men."

"Are you going to date other women?" she asked.

"No!" The certainty in his tone surprised her.

"So are you saying you want us to be exclusive?" Mindy couldn't conceal the hopeful note in her voice. She'd never been one to date around, or sleep around for that matter.

"If that's okay with you," he said, suddenly sounding less confident.

Mindy kissed his chin. "We could always give it a try. If it doesn't work out, at least we'll know for sure."

"Glad you see it my way."

* * * * *

For Nic, there was no longer any other option. His wolf had marked her. Claimed her for its own. It was what every member of the Moonlight Kin waited for, but not all found.

She was his mate. The only woman he'd ever desire.

His elation was tempered by the knowledge that she didn't know what he was. How was he going to break the news to her without her wanting to get away from him?

He jerked one last time, then gradually deflated. He was still inside her. In a few more minutes, he'd be ready to go again. "I didn't hurt you, did I?"

"Hurt?" Mindy laughed. "Hurt isn't the word I'd use to describe what we did, but I'll admit you are an animal in the sack."

He flinched at how close to the truth she was.

"It's okay," she said. "The bite just surprised me." Mindy touched her neck. "I think you broke the skin."

He swept her hand into his own and brought her knuckles to his lips. Nic ran his tongue over each groove and then sucked her finger into his mouth. Her eyes widened, but she didn't pull away.

"Was the experience terrible?" he asked.

"Truth is, I kind of liked it," Mindy said. "Does that make me kinky?"

Nic chuckled. "Don't think so, but I'm glad you liked it," he said. "I didn't mean to bite so hard." It was a lie and the truth. Nic might not have intended to mark her when they first climbed into bed, but he hadn't exactly pushed his wolf down when it rose. "I'm afraid you're going to have quite a hickey."

Mindy's gaze locked on him. "Really? I've never had one of those."

"Never?" he asked, astonished.

She shook her head. "Never. My mom and dad would've killed me."

Nic chuckled and kissed her on the chin. "It's nice to know that I'm the only one who's ever marked you." He sighed. "I don't want to ruin the moment, but I have an early morning tomorrow." He needed to report to Aidan and tell him what had happened. Biting was serious business. It was never done casually because of the repercussions.

"You don't want to stay?" she asked.

"I'd love to, but if I do neither one of us will get any sleep tonight." He gave her a wolfish grin.

Mindy smiled back him. "I can't be mad when you look at me like that."

"Like what?" He slipped out of her.

"Like a naughty little boy who uses his cuteness to get out of trouble."

He leaned over and helped her up. "You think I'm cute?"

Mindy rolled her eyes. "You're gorgeous and you know it."

Nic knew he wasn't gorgeous, but it was nice that she thought so. He pulled on his clothes and saw a pink robe hanging on the back of the door. He grabbed it and held it open for Mindy. She slipped it on and secured it at her waist.

"Walk me to the door," he said.

When they stepped out into the hall, Nic caught the elusive odor again. It was stronger here. Stronger than it had been before. He didn't like it. The scent made his hackles rise.

"Do you have any other pets?" he asked.

"No, why?" she asked.

"I just..." He couldn't exactly tell her that he'd smelled something. "Just curious."

"Nope," she said. "You've met everyone."

They walked to the door. "Thank you for dinner and"— he grinned—"everything else."

"Thank you for everything else." She looked at him. The emotion he saw swimming in her brown eyes laid him low.

"When can I see you again?" Nic didn't want to wait. Now that his wolf had marked her, he wanted to be around her as much as possible. She wasn't officially his bondmate until he completed the ritual and had her take his blood, but as far as he and his beast were concerned, Mindy was theirs.

"How about tomorrow night?"

"Sounds good." He pulled her into his arms and kissed her swollen lips, tasting her one last time before releasing her. "I really have to go or you're going to end up on your back again. Though I'm not against using the wall."

Mindy pressed her lips together.

"Sleep well," he said.

"You too."

Nic stepped out onto her front porch. "See you tomorrow."

"Bye." Mindy slowly shut the front door.

Nic didn't move until he heard her throw the lock. The second she did, he covered the ground between her house and his truck. He refused to look back. Didn't dare.

It was taking every ounce of his strength to walk away. He inhaled to clear his head, and caught the strange scent on the wind. What was it? And why was it at Mindy's home?

He glanced at the house. Mindy had turned the lights off and there was no movement near the curtains. Nic decided to investigate.

He climbed into his truck and started the engine. Nic backed out of her driveway. He didn't plan to go far. Just down the road, so he could park his truck out of sight. He wanted to scout the area around Mindy's house without her knowing about it. It was the only way he'd be able to sleep tonight.

Nic found a place to pull over and stepped out of his truck. He lifted his head, allowing his wolf to surface.

It didn't take long to find the unfamiliar odor. He tracked it to the edge of the woods, where it simply disappeared. It wasn't possible. Scents faded, but they didn't disappear. Before he could figure out the puzzle, a new odor replaced the old one. This was one Nic was beginning to hate. He swore under his breath. *Some pups never learn.*

First her job and now back to her home. It shouldn't have surprised him given Weres' competitive natures, but Nic was astonished. Mindy had asked them to leave, and so had he.

The brazen one knew he'd slept with her. He'd smelled Mindy on his skin. There was only one way her scent could've gotten there.

Nic let out a loud growl, warning the Weres to stay away, telling them without words that Mindy was off limits. Now that his wolf had claimed her, Nic was done playing with them.

If they jumped him or if either showed up at Mindy's house again, he'd consider it a direct challenge to his position in the pack. If that happened, they wouldn't be walking away.

Chapter Fourteen

Celina came home around ten o'clock and saw that she'd missed a call. She retrieved the message and heard Mindy's voice.

Her fingers tightened on the phone as Celina listened to the recording that confirmed her worst fears. Slade had been at Mindy's house. The message ended and she hung up.

Celina needed to call Mindy back and tell her the truth about what was going on. She'd chickened out of telling her earlier at work because Mindy had been so happy about her date with Nic. But now...

She punched in the number.

Slade walked into the apartment and slammed the door behind him. "Hang up the phone." The quiet intensity of his voice warned her not to argue.

Celina put the phone down. "Mindy called. She said that the hybrid was over at her house. She knows that I lied. It's only a matter of time before she finds out the truth," she said. "What were you doing over there?"

"Nothing," he snarled.

"Slade, don't lie to me," she said. "I've seen how you look at her. I'm not blind and I'm not stupid."

"You don't know what you're talking about." He moved deeper into the tattered apartment.

Celina hadn't imagined the attraction. She was hyper-aware of things like that. "Two Weres showed up at the clinic today after you left. They were sniffing after Mindy. She needs to know the truth," she said.

Hopefully it would scare her enough to make her want to have nothing to do with any of them. Maybe it would scare Mindy so much she'd leave town to join Izzy in New Orleans.

"Who were they?" he asked softly.

"Marco Faretti and some guy named Nic," she said. "It doesn't really matter. All that's important is that I warn her and that you stay away from her. I don't want you getting hurt."

"The Moonlight Kin are interfering with my plans," Slade said. "They have to be stopped."

Plans? "What do you mean?" she asked.

His claws slipped out as he waved off her question. "You're not going to tell your friend anything. And you're definitely not going to run her out of town," he said. "I'd be very unhappy with you, Celina, if you did that."

Celina ran a hand through her long brown hair. "I don't understand what makes Mindy so special. Why are the wolves circling her?"

"I wouldn't expect you to understand. You're human," Slade said.

"So is Mindy," Celina hissed.

"True, for now," he said. "Not all humans are created equal."

What was that supposed to mean? Didn't she give him everything that he needed? Didn't she cater to his every whim? What more did he want?

"What I desire you cannot give me," Slade said, his amber eyes glistening.

Panic struck swift and deep, sweeping aside her fear of

him invading her mind. "How do you know unless you tell me what you need? Mindy is inexperienced. She doesn't even know your kind exists. She can't give you what you want, but I can."

He focused his fierce attention on her and stalked forward. "Can you? That's quite a boast, since you don't know what I want," he said.

"Yes, I do," she murmured.

"Are you absolutely certain?" Slade asked.

Celina nodded. "Yes," she said, backing up until she hit the wall.

Slade tilted his head and sniffed her neck.

She whimpered. Would this finally be the moment he claimed her? Marked her as his own? Celina trembled in anticipation.

A secretive smile canted his lips, then disappeared. "You know nothing about our kind," he said.

"I know everything important," Celina responded.

Slade laughed and grabbed her by the waist. He turned her away from him until Celina faced the wall. Claws scraped against her bare skin.

"Careful," she said. "You almost scratched me."

He ran his thumbs over the faded scars that marred her hips and lower back. "It's quite a collection of scratch marks you have here. I doubt one more set would be noticed."

Celina sobbed. "They meant nothing to me." It was a lie. "You know I love only you." She waited, hoping he'd return the sentiment, but silence met her. Crushed, Celina tried to move his hands away from the evidence of her other dalliances.

Slade's fingers tightened, almost to the point of pain. "Don't," he said, then stripped her jeans away.

Dressed only in her shirt and panties, Celina quivered in anticipation.

Slade pressed a kiss on her nape, then tore her underwear off.

She heard the hiss of a zipper. His jeans brushed against the back of her legs as they dropped to his knees.

Slade placed his hand between her shoulder blades and pressed down until she bent at the waist. He dipped a thick finger inside her. Celina whimpered and drove her hips back to push him deeper.

He smacked her bottom and tsked. "Behave or I won't give you what you want."

Celina swallowed hard and concentrated on slowing her breathing. She wanted him. Wanted this. *Wanted to be one of them.* She'd put up with his heavy-handed ways to achieve her dream.

The thick bulbous head slid between her thighs and parted her. Celina bit her lip. She'd been with a lot of wolves over the years, but never one as dominant as Slade.

Sure, he scared her sometimes, but that was to be expected given his feral nature. It didn't change how she felt about him or what she wanted from him.

"Please, Slade." Celina wiggled her bottom.

He laughed, the sound mirthless. "I had no idea humans could be so easily controlled."

"They aren't." Celina tried to keep from groaning as he slipped an inch inside her. Slade was so big, so thick, so incredibly hard. Her body craved him, while her thoughts bordered on mania.

The first time he'd taken her, she'd blacked out from the pleasure. In that moment, an addiction had formed. An addiction so powerful that she couldn't imagine ever breaking the habit.

"You won't get over me, unless I want you to," he murmured against her ear, then latched on to her lobe.

"You're pretty sure of yourself," she said.

Slade chuckled. "No, Celina, I'm sure of you," he whispered.

What did that mean? Before she could give it anymore thought, he thrust hard, burying himself inside her.

There was no gentleness in his taking. Slade slammed into her, rocking Celina onto her toes as he worked her body into a frenzy.

"Yes!" she screamed as he pounded her, his strong hands holding her tight and guiding her back to meet every thrust.

"I don't appreciate having my actions questioned, Celina," he said, spearing her deep. "Do you understand?"

She groaned. "Yes."

He reached around her body and found her hidden bundle of nerves. Instead of stroking it, Slade pinched her hard.

Celina sucked in a startled breath, then mewed. Her knees wobbled, then buckled beneath her. Slade caught her before she hit the floor, and held her up. He didn't break rhythm once as he continued to ride her.

"I want your word that you won't reveal the truth to Mindy. Do you hear me?" He shook her lightly. "You have no idea what's happening here."

Celina's mind was in meltdown. She couldn't focus on anything but the pleasure-filled pain of their coupling.

"Your word, Celina. I'll have it now!" He pressed down and his thumb twitched at such a speed that the breath left her lungs. He was thrusting so fast that she couldn't track his movements. It was a not-so- subtle reminder that he wasn't human.

"Say it!" Slade demanded.

He was asking her to choose between him and her friendship with Mindy. She couldn't do it.

Slade snarled and pumped harder.

Celina came apart in his arms. In the end, the decision was far too easy. "I'll do whatever you want," she gasped.

"Promise?" he asked, as he rutted like a beast.

"I swear!" Celina cried as shockwaves rocked her.

"Good girl." Slade stroked the soft curls at her apex, then gave them a quick pat. He wrapped another arm around her waist and lifted Celina off her feet, moving her boneless body around until she was draped over the arm of the couch.

At this angle, every thrust struck her heart. Slade impaled her, driving his point in over and over. Skin slapped skin as he picked up his pace once more.

Celina wanted him to empty himself inside her. Fill her womb with life. She'd stopped using birth control, but hadn't told him yet. She knew it was wrong to withhold that kind of information, but Celina was desperate and determined to keep Slade any way she could—even if that meant trapping him with a child.

She didn't see Slade's sly smile, but Celina heard him snort.

"You are so predictable, sweetheart," he said. "You almost make it too easy." Slade thrust a few more times, then grunted and emptied himself inside her.

CHAPTER FIFTEEN

Mindy awoke bright and early the next morning, feeling deliriously happy. Despite their unorthodox start, she and Nic had reached a turning point last night.

She glanced over to the spot he'd been lying in earlier and was surprised to see a flower had been placed on the pillow, along with a note. When had Nic come back? How had he gotten in? Why didn't he wake her?

Mindy picked the items up and smelled the bloom. She put the rose by her bedside, then opened the note. She grinned as she read it.

Had a great time last night. Promise I'm not a stalker. Just wanted to see you once more. Couldn't bring myself to wake you. You looked too peaceful. Make sure all your windows are locked before you go to bed tonight. I'll call you later. Can't wait to see you. Nic

Mindy grabbed his pillow and brought it to her nose. She inhaled. His clean, rugged scent lingered on the pillowcase. Mindy groaned.

"You have it bad, girl," she murmured, then laughed.

She stretched, feeling the sore muscles in her body. Nic had been voracious last night and so had she. Obviously she was working hard to overcome her dry spell. Mindy giggled and threw the duvet cover back. She heard whimpers coming from outside her door.

"I'll be there in a minute, guys. Let me grab a shower first."

Mindy showered and got ready quickly. Nic hadn't been kidding about that hickey. No amount of makeup would conceal it. She threw on a fresh pair of jeans and an oversized T-shirt, then rushed into the hall. She didn't want Tart to have an accident.

She grabbed the leash and quickly took the three-legged poodle out into the backyard to do her business. The sun had just crested the trees and the air was crisp and only hinting at the heat to come.

Once her dog was finished, Mindy led her back into the house and proceeded to feed the gang. Hannibal glared at her, but didn't turn his nose up at the moist offering.

Mindy stroked his head. "I'm sorry, buddy, but it was either you or Nic, and I just couldn't turn his offer down."

Hannibal sniffed and turned his butt toward her. "Fine." Mindy ignored her finicky cat and grabbed the jar of crickets she kept under the sink. "Sorry, guys," she said as she walked over to George's aquarium and sprinkled a few in with him.

She sealed the jar and placed it back under the sink. She'd just closed the cabinet when the phone rang. Mindy picked up the receiver, hoping to hear Nic's baritone voice on the other end of the line. Instead, it was Izzy.

"Mindy, are you okay?" Izzy asked. Zydeco music blared in the background.

What time was it in New Orleans? "Izzy, I can barely hear you. Where are you?"

"It doesn't matter," Izzy said. "You need to listen to me. You're in danger."

Mindy frowned. "What?"

"Darkness is closing in," she said. "The spirits told me."

She sighed. "Izzy, I don't know what that means." Mindy's great mood was slowly beginning to sour. This was one aspect of their relationship that she didn't miss.

"Just be careful," Izzy said. "He's close."

Did she mean Marco Faretti?

Mindy's heart pounded. She wasn't ready to go another round with Marco right now. She peeked out the curtains at her driveway, but didn't see any other car but hers. She let the curtain drop.

"Who's close?" Mindy asked, losing patience. "I need more information."

One zydeco song ended and another began. "I have to go," Izzy said.

"Not yet!" Mindy shouted. "Not until you explain what you mean."

"Just remember what I told you," Izzy said, then hung up.

Mindy cursed and stared at the phone. "As usual, you didn't say anything," she muttered.

She knew better than to be drawn into these conversations. Hadn't she learned her lesson a long time ago?

"I love you, but you're not going to ruin my day," she said, then placed the phone back on its cradle.

Mindy grabbed her keys and backpack, then stepped out onto the porch. "Behave yourselves," she said, then locked the front door.

She turned her face up to the sun, allowing the warmth to soak into her skin and chase the shadows away. Mindy smiled and skipped down the stairs.

As she stepped off the bottom one, her foot tangled on something solid and Mindy lost her balance. Her backpack went flying as she put her hands out to break her fall.

Mindy landed with a hard thud, scraping her palms. She hissed and rubbed the bleeding cuts onto her jeans, then checked to see what she'd stumbled over.

For a moment, Mindy's brain couldn't make sense of what she was seeing. When the picture finally registered, she scrambled back.

The pale, lifeless body had been mangled by something. Big chunks of flesh were missing from the chest and arms. His throat gaped open like his mouth. She forced herself to concentrate on the man's face.

"Please," she whimpered, praying it wasn't Nic.

Her horror intensified when she saw who was lying at the bottom of her front steps. Mindy's stomach lurched. It couldn't be. Oh no. She had to still be asleep.

Please let me be dreaming.

But Mindy knew she wasn't. The pain in her hands and knees was real. So was her sister's cryptic warning. She stared at the terror-stricken dead body of Marco Faretti. Nic's promise from last night came rushing back. He'd said he would take care of him. Was this what he meant?

Izzy had said he was close. You don't get much closer than when you sleep with someone.

I can't breathe. I can't breathe.

Mindy's heart hurt and her lungs burned. She couldn't be wrong about Nic. She just couldn't be. Izzy had to be mistaken. The euphoria she'd experienced a minute ago faded and doubts crept in. Mindy struggled to her feet.

She had to call the police, but what was she going to say? She didn't want to get Nic in trouble, but she couldn't lie. Not about something like this.

What if he *had* hurt Marco? Mindy didn't want to believe it. She'd always trusted her instincts. They'd never led her astray, but what if she was wrong and Izzy was right? No one else knew about Marco hassling her, except Nic and Celina. And there was no way Celina could've done this kind of damage. She wasn't sure how Nic could've caused these types of injuries.

Marco looked like he'd been ripped apart, starting from

the throat all the way down through his intestines.

Could the hybrid have done this? He'd never shown any signs of aggression and there were no drag marks by the body. If the hybrid had attacked Marco, there'd be drag marks.

Why hadn't Tart barked when this was happening? Why hadn't she heard anything? The lack of noise meant Marco hadn't been killed here. He'd been dumped onto her sidewalk.

Would Nic do something like that knowing that she'd find the body? It seemed unlikely, but Mindy couldn't immediately come up with a better explanation.

Mindy's fingers trembled as she pulled her phone out of her pocket. The pain in her chest increased as she dialed 911.

She couldn't look at Marco any more. If she did, she was going to be sick. Mindy gave him a wide berth as she walked around the house to the back door and let herself in. She'd wait in here for the police. She saw Nic's business card on the kitchen counter and felt tears sting her eyes.

* * * * *

Nic smiled as the sun shone through his windshield. A cool breeze ruffled his hair as he drove into work. He'd overslept and was late for the first time in years, but Nic couldn't be upset because it was the best night's sleep he'd had in weeks. And he owed it all to Mindy MacDougal.

His grin widened as he thought about the woman who'd changed his life forever. There was still a lot to get past. Mindy would eventually have to learn the truth about him and the other Kin, but there was plenty of time to tell her.

Nic bounced in his seat as he turned down the hidden drive that led into the estate. He couldn't wait to tell Aidan the good news. Finding one's mate was cause for celebration amongst the Moonlight Kin. Nic looked forward to the hunt that would follow.

As he approached the security gate, Nic noticed that it was open. The skin on his neck prickled with unease. The gate was never left open. Alpha's orders. Nic continued down the long, tree-lined drive. As he drew nearer, he could hear voices and a commotion.

The trees parted and the estate came into view, along with a half-dozen police cars. Their lights were flashing, but their sirens were off.

What was going on?

Nic parked and turned off his engine. He'd just stepped out of the vehicle when he was approached by two officers. They asked him his name and told him to state his business.

Nic saw Aidan standing next to the front door. The Alpha looked at him and frowned.

"It's him," one of the officers who'd asked his name said.

"What's going on?" Nic asked.

An older police officer with thinning red hair and world-weary eyes stepped forward. "I'm Detective Markinson and that's Detective Daniels."

Though similar in age to Nic, Daniels' narrow face and jerky movements made him look like an over-caffeinated ferret.

"We'd like to ask you a few questions," Markinson said.

"About what?" Nic asked.

"It would be better if you could come down to the station and answer them there," Markinson said.

Nic's anxiety increased. "First I'd like to know what this is all about."

Aidan approached with a short mustached gentleman trotting along beside him. "This is Mr. La Croix's attorney. He'd like to have a word with his client before they follow you to the station."

It wasn't a request and both detectives knew it.

Markinson looked at Nic. "This is just a casual inquiry. Do you think you need an attorney present?"

Nic glanced at Aidan. The Alpha gave nothing away, but

he had his answer. "That might be best until I know what's going on here."

Neither cop looked happy, but Markinson nodded and said, "See you down at the station."

Aidan jerked his head toward the house. The second the office door closed, the Alpha descended upon Nic. "We don't have much time," Aidan said. "What in the hell is going on?"

Nic shook his head. "I don't know."

"Where were you this morning?" Aidan asked.

"I overslept."

"Those are homicide detectives," Aidan said.

Mindy...

Nic's stomach plummeted and pain ripped through his chest. Fur rippled over his arm as his wolf struggled to break free. Its first instinct was to get to its mate.

Aidan growled. "Pull yourself together. The last thing we need is for you to shift in front of the police."

Nic struggled to breathe. Struggled to think as his primal side rode him hard. "I have to get to Mindy."

"Who's Mindy?" Aidan asked.

Their gazes met and clashed. "My mate," Nic snapped.

Aidan's dark brow rose, disappearing beneath his long black hair. "When did this happen?"

"Last night," Nic bit out. "I'd planned to inform you this morning." His big body swayed and Nic gripped the back of a chair. "She can't be dead."

Aidan's face blanked. He immediately reached for the phone and punched in a number. "You have a body coming in," he said to the person on the other end of the line. "I want to know everything about it. You know what to do." He hung up. "You have to go down to the station now. Leave your cell phone here in case they jump the gun and book you. Whatever you do, don't incriminate yourself."

Hard to do when you don't know what's going on, Nic thought, and handed Aidan the phone.

"Report back here the second you're finished," Aidan said. "That's an order. I don't want you to take any detours. No side trips. Am I clear?"

Nic nodded, and they left.

* * * * *

The Breakbend police station was set up like every other small-town police force. There were only three rooms: one for the head of the department, one for interrogation, and the last for everyone else.

Five desks were slammed together, each housing an ancient-looking computer. A jail cell built for ten people max had been shoved into the corner, out of the way. The bars were a constant reminder of where you were, in case you forgot.

Nic and his attorney walked into the station and were immediately met by Detective Markinson. He led them into the interrogation room and asked them to take a seat. The red light on the camera mounted to the ceiling came on. Detective Daniels followed them into the room and shut the door behind him.

They'd barely settled in when the detectives fired off the first round of questions.

"Do you know a Ms. Mindy MacDougal?" Daniels asked.

Nic glanced at his attorney. The man nodded for him to answer.

"Yes, is she all right?" he asked.

Neither detective answered, which only alarmed Nic more.

"How long have you been seeing her?" Daniels asked.

Nic rubbed the back of his neck. "We just met the other night."

"Have you slept with her?" Daniels asked.

Nic's jaw clenched. "I don't see how that is any of your business."

"We'll take that as a yes," Daniels said and glanced at Markinson.

"Do you know a Marco Faretti?" Markinson asked.

He hadn't. At least not until the other night. Nic didn't like where this was going. "Not personally," he said.

"But you do know who he is," Daniels said.

"Yes, I've seen him around recently," Nic said. What did this have to do with Mindy?

"I believe you've done more than see him," Daniels said. "Think hard."

"Is Mindy okay?" Nic asked again. He could barely keep his agitation under wraps. Had Marco hurt her?

"Why wouldn't she be?" Daniels asked.

"Please tell me. I need to know," Nic said. "Marco was hassling her the other night and stalking her at her job."

"Did you take care of him for her?" Markinson asked. "Did she ask for your help?"

The questions surprised Nic. "What's that supposed to mean?" He shifted in the hard seat, trying to get comfortable.

"She's a pretty girl," Daniels said. "I can see how a guy could lose his head over her and do something stupid. Something he might regret later."

The wolf rose before Nic could stop it. He knew the detective was baiting him, but he didn't like him using Mindy, using his mate.

"I don't know what you're talking about. I admit that I got into a scuffle with Marco at a bar. A scuffle he started, I might add. The next day I asked him to leave Mindy alone," he said. "That's the extent of my contact with him."

"How long have you lived in the area?" Markinson asked.

"Eleven years," Nic said.

"So you're familiar with the back roads and the woods," Markinson said.

Nic was more than familiar with the woods in the area, but he didn't think it was a good idea to let them know it. "I'm familiar with the roads I travel on regularly. As for the woods, I only go into them during hunting season.”

“Are you sure you didn’t run into him again?” Daniels asked, changing the subject. “Maybe he was sniffing around your girlfriend? Maybe she invited him over in between your visits? Ever think of that?”

Nic bared his teeth. “Get to the point.”

His attorney put his hand on Nic’s shoulder and squeezed. It was a warning to get his wolf under control.

“Mr. Faretti was found murdered on the steps of Ms. MacDougal’s home this morning,” Daniels said.

Nic shot to his feet. “What! Is Mindy okay? How long has he been dead?” What he really wanted to know was how he died. Marco might be a pup, but he was still a shifter. Weres didn’t go down easily.

“We’re trying to ascertain that now,” Daniels said.

“As you can see by his explosive reaction to the news, Mr. La Croix had no idea that Mr. Faretti was dead,” Nic’s attorney said.

“Where were you this morning between three o’clock and six o’clock?” Daniels asked.

“In bed. Asleep,” Nic said.

“Can anyone verify that?” Markinson asked.

Nic shook his head. “No,” he said, “I was alone.”

“So what you’re saying is that you don’t have an alibi,” Daniels said.

“What I’m saying is I don’t need one,” Nic replied.

Daniels snorted. “For your sake, I hope you’re right.”

They continued questioning Nic, doing a variation of good cop, bad cop until he reached the end of his tether.

“Listen, I have told you everything I know. Asking me the same questions over and over isn’t going to change my answers,” Nic said.

“Mind if we get your fingerprints and DNA?” Markinson asked.

“Sorry, gentleman, but I’m not going to allow my client to participate in a fishing expedition,” the attorney said. “Mr.

La Croix has been more than cooperative, especially since the coroner hasn't had time to determine the cause of death yet. If you have any further questions for Mr. La Croix, please direct them to me." The attorney glanced at Nic. "Let's go."

Daniels scowled at the lawyer. Markinson didn't look at all surprised.

"We'll be in touch," Markinson said. "In the meantime, don't leave town."

"Hadn't planned to," Nic said. He was still trying to process what he'd been told. In the end, all that mattered to him was that Mindy was still alive.

Nic and his attorney returned to the estate. The interrogation had taken two hours. Two hours that were better spent checking on Mindy. The need to rush to her side was almost unbearable. The attorney ushered him into Aidan's office.

"Take a seat," Aidan said, then glanced at the attorney. "What happened?"

"Marco Faretti was murdered, or at least that's what they suspect right now," the lawyer said.

"Do they have any proof?" Aidan asked.

The attorney shook his head.

"Then why did they think you did it?" Aidan asked Nic.

"I guess I'm the most obvious suspect." Nic scrubbed a hand over his face. Mindy must be scared out of her mind. "Can I have my phone back?"

"What for?" Aidan asked.

"I want to call Mindy," he said. "Make sure she's okay."

"No!" Aidan snapped. "I don't want you talking to her. I don't want you anywhere near her until we know what's going on."

"She's my mate," Nic ground out. "That's not going to happen."

Aidan sat back, eyeing him closely. "I know there's been some tension between us. I hope that doesn't have anything to do with this current situation."

"It doesn't," Nic said.

"I take it your new mate is human," Aidan said. The answer was obvious, since no Kin would call in the human authorities over the death of one of their own.

Nic's jaw clenched.

"Does she know what you are?" Aidan asked.

"No," Nic said.

"That could be a problem," Aidan said.

"It wasn't for *your* mate," Nic snarled and glared at Aidan in direct challenge.

Aidan's amber eyes glowed until they were molten gold, and his incisors lengthened. He growled deep in his chest and rose to his feet. As he stared at Nic, the sound grew louder.

Nic didn't want to challenge the Alpha for his position. He wasn't interested in leading the pack. The only thing he wanted was to get to his mate's side to protect her. Nic forced his gaze down until he stared at the beige carpet.

Aidan continued to growl, then slowly sat back down. "You only get one pass," he said. "The next time you do that, I'll rip your throat out."

Nic swallowed hard. "Understood, Alpha."

Aidan clasped his hands together. "Now, I'm going to ask you one time and one time only," he said. "Did you kill the pup?"

Nic looked him in the eye. "No."

"Do you know who did?" Aidan asked.

"No idea," Nic said.

"Did they say how he was killed?" Aidan asked.

"No." Nic shook his head. "They were pretty tight-lipped about the details. Didn't give much out."

Aidan crossed his arms over his wide chest. "I should be getting a call from the coroner soon," he said. It paid to have wolves in the right positions. "Until I do, can you handle this situation on your own or do I need to step in?"

Nic's eyes flared.

Aidan snarled.

The attorney took a step back so he was no longer next to them.

"I'll handle it," Nic said. "Let me know what they find out." He had to get out of Aidan's office before his wolf got them into more trouble. On his way out, Nic ran into Jenna.

"Is it true that there's been a murder?" she asked.

"According to the police."

Her face paled. "Do we know who it is?"

"Marco Faretti," he said.

Her pale brow furrowed. "I don't think I know him."

"He doesn't live in town," Nic said.

Jenna stared at him, tilting her head from side to side. "You look different," she said.

Some of the rage seeped out of him. "I am different," Nic said softly.

He no longer felt anything for Jenna beyond friendly affection and abiding respect. How could he have believed that she was meant for him? He should've listened to his wolf. It knew all along.

"I have to go," he said. "My mate needs me."

Nic heard her swift intake of breath as he strode down the hall to the front door.

Chapter Sixteen

Mindy skipped class, but decided to go to work. She couldn't bring herself to stay around the house all day knowing that Marco's body had been lying outside at the bottom of her front steps.

She left out her back door and walked around the house. There was a crimson stain on the sidewalk where Marco had been. Her stomach soured as she climbed into her car.

She turned the key and the engine hummed smoothly. The lack of a ping reminded her that Nic had been there only a few hours earlier and they'd shared one of the best nights of her life.

Sadness rose inside of her. Where was Nic and what was he doing? Had the police contacted him yet? Had they arrested him? Would he ever forgive her if they had?

Mindy thought about Izzy's cryptic warning. She'd thought for sure her sister had been talking about Marco, but now...

She backed out of her driveway and drove into town. By the time Mindy reached Breakbend, her eyes were rimmed with red and her face was blotchy from crying. She parked behind the clinic and let herself inside. The cheerful light blue walls and photographs of satisfied customers did little to ease her pain.

Celina took one look at her and jumped out of her seat. "What happened? What's wrong? Did Nic do this?" she asked. "Is Izzy okay?"

Mindy sniffled and more tears appeared. "It's Marco."

Celina drew back in confusion. "Marco? What about Marco? I thought you didn't want anything to do with him. I told you that he was bad news."

Celina's face swam before Mindy's eyes. "He's dead," Mindy said. "I found his body on my sidewalk."

"What!" Celina shouted. "What happened?"

Mindy shook her head. "He was killed. Torn apart by something or someone. It was awful."

Celina's eyes widened. "When?"

"Sometime last night," she said. "I didn't hear anything."

"How?" Celina asked.

"I don't know," Mindy said. "He had to have been killed somewhere else and dumped in front of my house. Who would do that?"

Celina paled. "Oh, honey, are you okay?" She pulled Mindy into her arms and hugged her tight.

Mindy sniffed. "I don't know. I think I'm still in shock."

Celina reached for the box of tissues on her desk and handed them to Mindy. "I know you're scared, but why are you crying? This is Marco we're talking about. He was a jerk, remember?"

"I know, but I didn't want him dead," Mindy wailed.

"Did Nic spend the night?" Celina asked.

Mindy shook her head.

"Did you call him to let him know about Marco?" Celina asked.

"I can't," Mindy sobbed.

"Why not?" Celina asked.

"Because I had to tell the police about him and Marco getting into a fight the other night," Mindy said.

Celina pulled back. "Do you think Nic hurt Marco?"

Tears flowed down Mindy's cheeks. "Izzy called to warn me this morning. She was totally freaking out."

"To warn you about what?" Celina asked.

"Danger being nearby," Mindy said. "I don't know what to think anymore."

* * * * *

Celina studied her friend's blotchy face and tear-stained cheeks. She didn't look injured. Her gaze wandered lower until it reached a dark, angry smudge on the side of Mindy's neck.

At first she couldn't figure out what she was looking at. "What happened to your neck?" Celina moved Mindy's shirt aside to get a better look.

Mindy's hand shot up and covered the spot, but not before Celina saw the teeth marks in the wound.

"Nic got carried away last night and gave me a hickey," she said.

Celina's heart dropped. "Is that what he said it was?"

"What else would it be?" Mindy asked.

What else indeed...

In Celina's experience, wolves didn't get carried away. There were no accidents when it came to marking a female. They took mating very seriously and they never bit a neck without it meaning something.

"Take a seat," she said. "I'm going to get you a cup of tea, then I want you to start from the beginning and tell me everything. Okay?"

Mindy nodded. "Okay."

Celina's hands shook as she walked into the small kitchenette to make Mindy a cup of tea. That wasn't a hickey on her neck. A hickey wouldn't have broken the skin. It also wouldn't have teeth marks. Mindy was too naïve to know otherwise.

Nic had marked her. His *wolf* had marked her. In the eyes of the pack, Mindy was now one of them. How could this have happened? He'd only known her for a few days.

Resentment roiled inside Celina. Such a waste. The idiot didn't understand the significance of the mark. Couldn't appreciate the honor that had been bestowed upon her because she didn't know that the Moonlight Kin existed.

Celina tossed the ceramic cup into the sink, shattering it. She gripped the side of the sink and stared at the broken shards. It wasn't fair.

"Are you okay?" Mindy asked.

Celina bit the inside of her mouth, using the pain to focus her. "I'm fine," she said. "Just clumsy. I'll be right out with your tea."

If Slade hadn't made her promise not to tell Mindy the truth, she'd march into the other room right this instant and set her straight. But he had, so she couldn't.

Celina picked up another cup and put in a tea bag. While the tea steeped, she thought about Slade. He'd been hinting at marking her, but had put the act off repeatedly.

She had tried to be patient, tried to give him the time and space he needed, but seeing Mindy's mark brought clarity to her mind that hadn't existed before. Celina was done waiting.

Tonight, she'd push Slade for a commitment. If he balked, she'd tell him about Mindy's mark and ask him to move out.

Mind made up, Celina picked up the cup of tea and took it to Mindy. "This should make you feel better," she said, but her thoughts had already returned to Slade and the upcoming discussion they would have.

CHAPTER SEVENTEEN

The only reason anyone would leave a dead body lying on someone's front lawn was if they meant to send a message.

The question was, who was the warning for? Him? Or Mindy?

It seemed more likely the warning had been meant for him, but Nic couldn't rule out the chance that it was meant for her. What could anyone possibly warn Mindy about?

He sped to her house, determined to check on her and make sure she was okay. Once he assured himself that she was unharmed, he'd sniff around to see what he could pick up. The cops were good, but their noses couldn't match one of the Kin's.

Nic was surprised to find Mindy's car gone when he arrived. Where could she be? He hadn't seen her at the police station. He didn't think she'd go to school or work, not after finding a body.

Mindy's car wasn't the only thing missing. The police were gone, too, but the crime-scene tape still surrounded the area near her front porch.

Nic rolled down his window and sniffed the air. He

needed to make sure he was alone before he pulled over. Other than a few deer in the distance, he didn't detect anything of size. He guided the truck over to the side of the road and put it in park, then slipped out of the cab.

He listened to the sound of the wind. Nic stood perfectly still while the woods whispered their secrets. As soon as he was sure it was safe, he loped over to Mindy's yard and scented the area.

Death hit him instantly. It clung to the grass and soiled the dirt with its foul odor. The coppery scent of blood followed on death's heels. Marco may have been a pain in the ass, but he didn't deserve to die.

Nic slowly circled the area, sniffing every few feet to make sure he didn't miss anything. As he moved further out, he caught the elusive scent that had bothered him before. It was all over the yard. The strongest concentration hung in the air where the body had been. His wolf bristled. Nic followed the odor toward the woods.

Before he could reach the trees, Nic came across an odd *stain*. He circled the spot, smelling every inch of the diameter. The stain wasn't blood. Wasn't chemical. And it definitely wasn't man made.

Nic crouched down to examine the spot. He dipped a finger into the residue. The second the ashy substance hit his skin, it burned like acid. Nic ignored the pain long enough to sniff his finger. The stench of magic filled his nostrils and he stumbled back, landing on his butt.

It wasn't possible. Couldn't be. They were myth. Legends created to scare children into behaving.

There was only one creature Nic had heard of that left that kind of stain behind, and as far as he knew, it wasn't real.

The hair on the back of his neck rose, warning him that he was being watched. Nic didn't react. Instead, he wiped the ash off his finger, ignoring the blisters it had left behind.

Nic slowly scanned the area with his senses and

detected—*nothing*. He rose to his feet. For the first time in his life, Nic knew what it felt like to be prey. He didn't like the sensation one bit and neither did his wolf.

He left the stain and headed toward his truck. Not once did Nic take his eyes off the woods, until he drove away. The idea that the bogeyman might be after Mindy terrified Nic and left him shaken. If he hadn't been certain about his growing feelings for her before, the deadly threat solidified them.

What had she gotten herself into? It was more imperative than ever that he find her. If what Nic had discovered was real, then Mindy wasn't safe. No one was.

* * * * *

Mindy nearly fell out of her seat when Nic burst into the animal clinic. Seeing him in person only added to her sense of guilt and confusion. She'd spent the morning at the police station giving them her statement. She'd had no choice but to tell them about Nic. That didn't mean she felt good about the decision.

His face was flushed and he was out of breath. His big body tensed when he saw her. She expected him to start yelling any second.

"Are you okay?" he asked.

The question surprised her. Didn't he want to know why she'd given the police his name?

Nic's gaze roamed over her, settling for a breath or two on her hickey before moving on.

"I'm fine," she said, finally finding her voice. "I'm sorry. I had no choice. I had to tell them."

"Doesn't matter," Nic said. "I'm just glad you're all right. I was so worried when the police stopped by my workplace and told me there'd been a murder. They didn't tell me who died." He pulled her into his arms and held her close. "I thought I'd lost you." Nic's voice cracked.

Mindy pushed out of his embrace. "I didn't want to get you into trouble, but I couldn't lie."

He grabbed her hand, threading his fingers between hers. "There's nothing to apologize for. You did the right thing."

"You're not mad?" She'd be mad if she were in his shoes.

Nic smiled. "No, honey. I'm relieved."

She stared at him. "It was horrible." Her voice quivered.

"I can imagine. I'm sorry you had to go through something like that alone," Nic said. "I wish I could've been there for you. I should've been there. I won't let you down again." His body quaked. "If only he had been there when I left."

"He wasn't?" Mindy asked, watching his face closely.

"No!" Nic frowned. "I would've noticed a dead body."

He took a deep, exasperated breath and his expression changed. Fury replaced concern. The switch was so abrupt that it left Mindy shaking. Nic gently moved her aside and rushed into the main part of the clinic.

"What are you doing?" she asked. "Nic, where are you going?" Mindy raced in after him.

Nic didn't stop until he reached the recovery area. Only a few animals were currently housed back there—a couple of dogs and two cats.

The second he entered the room, they all whimpered and clawed to get out of their cages. Nic ignored their reaction and moved deeper into the room. When he reached the largest cage, he crouched next to it.

"What happened to the animal inside this cage?" he asked. His tone was deadly serious. Mindy took a step back.

Celina came running into the room. Her eyes widened to the size of saucers when she saw Nic next to the empty cage.

Nic's gaze slid from Mindy to her friend. Rage returned, making it look like his blue eyes were glowing. "Where is it?" He pointed at the cage.

Celina's tawny face paled and her hand fluttered to her throat. "It's gone. I took it to a preserve and released it."

Mindy glanced at her. Why was Celina lying?

* * * * *

Nic could smell the lies emanating from Celina's skin. The sour odor stank up the room, but this was neither the time nor the place to confront her. Not in front of Mindy.

He should report to Aidan immediately. *And say what? I think the bogeyman is real?* Nic snorted. He wasn't about to present his findings to the Alpha until he had proof. An odd stain and a foul odor weren't enough. Not after everything that had happened this morning.

"Mindy, I think you should stay with me until the authorities find out who's responsible for Marco's death," he said.

Mindy slowly shook her head. "I can't do that."

Nic could see the fear shimmering in her brown eyes, smell it tainting her supple skin. And it broke his heart. "I know you're scared of me, especially after the morning you've had."

"I'm not scared," she said. "I just can't leave my animals alone."

He let her believe her own lies because Nic knew they were the only thing keeping her from falling apart. But there was no way he was going to leave her unprotected. She was his mate. It was his duty to take care of her. It was his honor, even if she didn't know it yet.

"Then you leave me no choice," Nic said. "I'll be over after you get off work."

Mindy's eyes widened. "Nic, you can't just barge into my life. A lot has happened. I need time to think."

"So you can convince yourself that I'm a murderer?" he asked. "I don't think so." Nic's gaze slid to Celina.

She took a step back.

"Tell her," he demanded. "You *know* she's safe with me. And you know why."

"She might," Mindy said. "But I don't."

Celina swallowed hard. "He's telling the truth," she said.

* * * * *

Mindy's head whipped around. She'd expected her friend to take her side of things. "How do you know?"

"I just do," Celina said.

"Well, forgive me if I don't take your word for it," she said.

"Mindy, someone left a body on your front lawn," Celina said. "Until we know who or what put it there"—she glared at Nic—"I don't want you being alone. Izzy would agree if she were here."

"But what if—"

"He didn't do it," Celina said. "Trust me."

"Do you know what you're asking?"

Celina sighed. "Yeah, I do," she said, glancing at Nic.

"Why do I feel like I'm not part of the conversation taking place?" Mindy asked.

Celina grabbed her hand. "Believe me, this is all about you," she said. "Nic had better protect you with his life."

"You know I will," he said, then sprang to his feet. He pressed a quick kiss on Mindy's mouth before she could protest, and strode out of the clinic.

Mindy watched him go, then glared at Celina. "Are you crazy? What if he killed Marco?"

Celina met her accusing gaze unflinchingly. "Do you believe that? Do you really believe that Nic is a murderer?"

Mindy opened her mouth to say yes, it was possible, but the words refused to come out. Her heart wouldn't let them. It just didn't believe that the same man who'd made love to her so tenderly, so passionately, had turned around the same night and killed a man. It didn't make sense.

Celina's gaze softened. "I know you haven't known him long, but I can tell you right now that he's serious about you.

He's committed more deeply than you can imagine." She touched Mindy's hickey, then pulled her hand away.

Mindy sighed. "A hickey doesn't mean anything," she said. "Last night we talked about being exclusive, but with everything that's happened I don't think that's a good idea."

"You're wrong," Celina said. "You saw how scared he was when he came in here. That's not something he could've faked. Nic *will* protect you. His kind redefines loyalty. If you don't believe me, call Izzy and ask."

"Izzy has never met Nic," Mindy said. "Has she?"

"No, but she'll still *know*," Celina said.

Mindy looked at her. Really looked. For the first time in all the years she'd known her, Celina appeared fragile. Was it because of Slade? Or was it something else?

Before she took a leap based on blind faith, there was one question she needed answered. "Why did you lie to Nic about the hybrid?"

Celina's gaze dropped and sadness etched her face. "You'll understand why soon enough." She sighed. "When you do, it'll be clear why I couldn't let anything happen to him," she said, and walked away.

Izzy wasn't the only one who spoke in riddles.

Chapter Eighteen

Nic showed up at Mindy's house like he'd promised, and knocked on her front door. Mindy opened it and stared at him. He had a black duffle bag slung over his shoulder and wore a stained white T-shirt with his blue jeans. His hair was tousled and he was grinning.

She almost smiled back, but stopped herself. "I still don't think this is a good idea," she said.

Nic studied her small porch and shrugged. "I don't have a problem sleeping right here," he said.

Mindy was tempted to let him, but then her gaze strayed to the crimson stain she hadn't quite been able to get off with her power hose. What if whoever killed Marco came back while Nic was on the porch?

Her heart thundered in her chest. She wouldn't be able to live with herself if anything happened to him. Mindy glared at him, but Nic's smile only widened. His eyes fixed on the hickey, and the strangest thing happened. The spot heated.

Mindy brushed her hand over it, and something in Nic's blue eyes flared. She stepped back. "Come in."

Nic walked into the living room and dropped his duffle bag next to the couch.

"Can I get you anything to drink?" she asked.

"Water," Nic said.

Mindy went into the kitchen to retrieve a bottle. When she returned, Nic was sprawled out across the couch, his wide shoulders and long legs eating up every square inch. He sat up when she handed him the water.

"Thanks," he said, then popped the cap and swallowed half the bottle in one gulp. "I know this isn't something you want to talk about, but I need to know if there's been anything strange going on lately."

"Define strange," she said. Her whole life was odd thanks to Izzy.

Nic set his bottled water down on the coffee table. "Let's start with the animal at the clinic," he said. "What was it and how did it get there?"

"It was a mutt. A big mutt, but a mutt nonetheless," she said. "I almost hit him with my car. When I first saw him, I thought he was dead."

"But it wasn't?"

Mindy shook her head. "No, but the animal was injured. Celina and I rushed it to the clinic, where Dr. Fields patched it up."

"What kind of mutt was it?" Nic asked.

"Wolf and something. Dr. Fields thought it had been bred with a Russian Bear dog, but the lab results were inconclusive," Mindy said. "Once it healed, Celina carted him off to the preserve."

Nic sat forward. "Are you sure?"

"As far as I know, that's what she did." Mindy couldn't meet his eyes when she was lying. Why was she protecting Celina, when her friend had tossed her to the wolves?

* * * * *

"Anything else unusual happen?" Nic asked. He didn't know why Mindy was lying, but he decided not to press her.

He was afraid if he did she'd shut down.

She thought about his question and shook her head. "Not really. I don't think Izzy's warning from the wind counts."

"What?" Nic asked. What did she mean by that?

She blanched. "Nothing," she said.

Nic touched her hand. "You can tell me. I won't laugh."

Mindy stared at him in indecision. Nic thought she would refuse to answer, then she took a deep breath and slowly let it out.

"Remember how I told you my sister was eccentric?" she asked.

Nic nodded.

"Well, there's a little bit more to the story than that." Mindy sank into the chair. "Truth is, Izzy is odd. It's not just her fascination with monsters."

Nic inwardly cringed, but kept his expression neutral. He didn't want Mindy to see what effect her words had on him. He needed her to continue talking.

"Sometimes Izzy knows things before they happen," Mindy said, and glanced away.

"Are you saying your sister is psychic?" Nic asked.

"I know it sounds crazy," she said. "You don't have to believe me, but she called this morning and warned me that darkness was near. She gave me the impression that I was in danger."

Nic's heart stuttered in his chest. "Did she say from who?"

Mindy shook her head. "That's the problem with Izzy and her visions. They aren't always clear," she said. "I know you don't believe me."

"Actually, I do," Nic said. Her sister was a Sighted-One. Is that why the Darkling was here? He shook his head. No, that didn't make sense, since her sister was gone. Unless... "Do you have the same abilities as Izzy?"

"No." She gave him a humorless laugh. "There was only room for one whack-a-doodle in the family."

Nic could sense her pain. "You said Izzy believed in monsters."

She nodded.

"What did you mean by that?" Nic asked.

"When we were kids, Izzy used to tell me crazy stories about monsters walking through the mall. Used to scare me to death. Eventually, I outgrew the stories, but Izzy never did," Mindy said. "She swore she could see them. She said they were everywhere. Izzy was always so scared. I think that's why she partied so much in her teens. But no amount of alcohol could make them or her visions go away."

It must've been terrifying for her, Nic thought. Growing up as a Sighted-One without any guidance had to be a lonely existence. Had loneliness also contributed to Mindy's isolation?

"I'd like to fix you some dinner," he said, clearly surprising her.

"You don't have to do that," she said.

"I know I don't have to," Nic said. "I want to. You just stay here and put your feet up." He didn't wait for her to answer. He simply walked into the kitchen.

* * * * *

Mindy watched him go. She'd expected Nic to laugh, when she'd told him about Izzy, but he hadn't. There'd been compassion in his eyes, and what looked like concern. She sat back and had just kicked her feet up when the doorbell rang.

"I'll get it," she said. Mindy glanced through the peephole, then opened the door. "Detective Daniels, what are you doing here?"

"I was in the neighborhood," he said. "Thought I'd stop by and make sure you were okay."

"Thank you," Mindy said. "I'm fine."

He shuffled his feet on her porch. "I just received the

coroner's report," he said.

Mindy's stomach dropped. This was it. What he said next could change everything. "What did it say?" she asked, not sure if she really wanted to know.

The detective watched her closely. "He ruled the death an animal attack. Said it most likely was a mountain lion."

"Really?" His answer shocked Mindy. Her surprise quickly morphed into relief. "I'm glad to hear Marco wasn't murdered."

The detective's lips thinned. It was evident that he didn't agree with the report. "I stopped by to tell you to be careful and to ask if you had anywhere else you could stay for a while. I don't like the idea of you being out here on your own," he said.

A hand grasped the side of the door, opening it wider. Nic appeared beside her shoulder. The detective stiffened and his brown eyes narrowed.

"She won't be alone," Nic said. "I'm here."

Detective Daniels gave him a hard cop stare, but Nic didn't seem intimidated in the least. The detective's gaze eventually returned to Mindy.

"You might want to take care with the crowd you're running with," he said. "Rumors around town say that the folks on the Fortier estate can be dangerous."

"I didn't think the police paid attention to gossip," Nic said, his voice lethal.

"Sometimes it pays to listen to whispers on the streets," Detective Daniels said. "You have a good night, Ms. MacDougal."

"You too."

* * * * *

Mindy shut the door. "That was weird."

"Did I hear him right? Did he say it was a mountain lion attack?" Nic asked.

"Yeah." Mindy's brow furrowed.

"But?" Nic asked, wondering why she didn't look convinced. "You don't believe him."

Mindy rubbed her neck. "No, I believe him. Why would he lie?"

"He wouldn't," Nic said, but the coroner would. "So what's bothering you?"

"Marco's body," she said. "How did it get in front of my house?"

"The cat must've dragged it there," he said.

Mindy stared at him. "That's just it. There weren't any drag marks."

Nic brushed her arm with his finger. "Are you sure? You were in shock when you found the body. Anybody would be. Is it possible you are mistaken?" He didn't want to put doubt in her mind, but Nic had no choice. The truth would have to stay buried until he could reveal all to her.

"I know I could be wrong, but I don't think I am." She rubbed her hands over her arms. "I know animals. Marco wasn't a little guy. Even a healthy-sized mountain lion would have had difficulty moving him. It would've had to drag him. If it couldn't, it would've sliced him open and eaten his stomach and intestines."

She was right. It wasn't a mountain lion that'd killed Marco. A cat couldn't take down a Were, but a Darkling could.

<h1 style="text-align:center">CHAPTER NINETEEN</h1>

Celina drove home without knowing how she got there. Her thoughts were too preoccupied with how she was going to confront Slade. She wanted that bond. If Mindy had one in such a short time period, then there was no reason for she and Slade to wait.

She pulled into the weathered apartment complex and parked in her numbered spot. Slade didn't have a car, so there was no telling if he was home yet. Celina hoped he wasn't. She wanted to get the apartment arranged into a romantic setting before he arrived.

What if he didn't come home tonight?

He'd been spending more and more time away. Celina wondered, not for the first time, if he'd changed his mind. She couldn't allow that to happen.

She remembered the fury on Nic La Croix's handsome face when he'd asked about Slade. His anger scared her. Why did Nic want to know where he was? Did it have anything to do with Marco's murder? Was it because Slade had been sniffing around Mindy's house? Or was it because he wasn't part of the Moonlight Kin?

Wolves were highly territorial. Couple that with Nic

leaving his mark on Mindy and you had a recipe for extreme violence.

A fresh wave of jealousy struck. Celina hated that Slade was so interested in Mindy, but she didn't want him harmed.

She got out of the car and walked to the tiny apartment she'd called home for the last few years. Gray paint peeled from the walls as she climbed the stairs to the second floor.

Celina opened the door and called out Slade's name. Her voice echoed in the silence. She didn't know how much time she had before he arrived, so she'd have to work fast.

She pulled out the candles from beneath her kitchen sink and lit them so that the warm glow softened the appearance of the tattered furniture.

Celina walked into her bedroom to search for her best lingerie. She placed the lacey outfit on the bed while she took a shower, then slipped it on beneath her jeans and green T-shirt. Celina went back into the kitchen and removed some chicken from the freezer so it had time to defrost.

Slade came home two hours later. He stopped in his tracks as he stepped through the front door. His gaze scanned the room, moving from the candles to the food on the table before settling on her.

"What's this?" he asked.

"I thought I'd do something nice for you," Celina said.

His amber eyes narrowed. "Why?"

"Do I need a reason?" Celina asked.

Slade smiled. "No, but I know you have one."

Celina exhaled. "Fine." She flipped on the lights.

"Do you know anything about a murder that occurred at Mindy's house last night?" she asked.

Slade glided deeper into the room, his molten eyes glittering.

"A body was dumped on her front lawn," Celina said. "She's terrified. Mindy came into work crying. I barely got her to calm down. I know I promised not to tell her, but I'm going to have to say something."

Slade shrugged as if it were inconsequential. "There is no reason for her to be afraid. No one's going to harm her."

"How do you know?" Celina asked. "Whatever killed Marco could still be lurking outside her house just waiting for an opportunity to get to her."

"Oh, I am certain it wants her. Just not for the reasons you suggest." He smiled.

"What's that supposed to mean?" she asked.

"People die every day, Celina. It's hardly a tragedy."

She put her hands on her hips. "You didn't answer my question."

"No." Slade laughed. "I didn't." He stalked around the apartment, moving as if he were caged and looking for a way out.

He hadn't denied anything, nor had he confessed. His evasive answers confused Celina and frightened her. Had he killed Marco? She didn't want to believe it, but Weres didn't live by the same laws as humans. She'd learned that over the years. Anyone familiar with the Moonlight Kin knew they were governed by a different set of rules. The punishment for breaking those rules was harsh. Had Slade broken the rules?

"You need to stay away from Mindy's house," she said. "It's not safe."

Slade's eyebrow arched. "I can't do that," he said.

"Why not?" Celina whined. Didn't the idiot understand that she was trying to save his life?

"Because I plan to claim her as my mate," Slade said casually.

"You can't do that!" Celina launched herself at him, pounding her fists on his chest.

Slade easily fended her off. "Stop it before you hurt yourself." He grabbed her wrists and pushed her down onto the couch until she was prone, then covered her body with his own.

"You promised," Celina gasped. "You said you'd claim

me.”

“I said no such thing,” Slade said.

He hadn't. Celina had heard what she'd wanted to hear. Slade had used her...just like all the other Weres.

“If you'd bothered to investigate before you spread your thighs for every wolf around, you'd know that claiming doesn't work like that,” he said.

“What do you mean?” She'd missed something. Something important. Something Slade had been aware of since day one. Anger replaced some of her pain.

“One sniff and I knew you weren't my mate. Most wolves can scent whether a woman is their mate or not,” he said. “There's a sweetness, a richness to her that runs beneath the surface.”

“So this whole time you've been playing me?” she asked.

“Don't take it personally,” Slade said. “In the beginning, I genuinely needed you.”

Celina glared at him, then smiled. “You're too late,” she hissed, thinking about Mindy's mark.

“What are you talking about?” Slade asked in confusion.

“You can't claim Mindy.” Celina laughed maniacally. She wasn't the only one who hadn't been paying attention. Celina couldn't wait to see the look on Slade's face when he found out the truth.

Slade bared his teeth. “Why not?” He shook her, but it only made her laugh harder.

Celina's smile returned, this time wider. “Because she's already been claimed.”

His amber eyes widened, then began to glow.

“That's right, Lover Boy, another wolf got to her first,” Celina said. “I saw the mark on her neck with my own eyes. It's kind of hard to miss. Did I forget to mention that the Were who marked her is looking for you?”

“Who? Who did it? Tell me now, you stupid bitch!” Slade snarled, slamming her against the couch cushions.

“Nic La Croix,” she said. “He's a big guy. I bet he's an

even bigger Were. He won't be as easy to take down as Marco."

Slade's eyes narrowed until only tiny slivers of gold were visible. "You think you're so clever. You think you know what's going on, but you don't know anything." As he pinned her to the couch, a single claw extended from his finger.

"What are you doing?" Celina asked. "Slade, talk to me."

"What's wrong, Celina?" he asked. "Since the moment I met you, you've been begging me to mark you. Change your mind?"

Her gaze fastened on the deadly claw. "Slade, honey, let's talk about this."

He shook his dark head. "There's nothing to talk about. I'm just giving you want you want," he said.

He was going to kill her. Celina could see it in his eyes. There was no warmth, no passion, only cold resolve. Celina struggled to break his grip.

"Slade, let me up. Stop playing around," she said.

He brought the claw to the inside of her wrist. If he sliced her the right way, it would look like a suicide and no one would suspect otherwise. Celina thought about Izzy's warning. She should've listened.

Slade ran the claw along her wrist, scratching her just deep enough for blood to surface on her skin. He leaned over and licked it off, then released her and rose from the couch. Slade walked toward the front door.

Celina was confused. She'd thought for sure that he was going to kill her. Maybe she was wrong about him? "Where are you going?" she asked.

"To get what I came to this world for," he said.

This world? What did he mean by that?

"You're just going to scratch me and leave?" Celina asked, though she no longer wanted him to stay.

"One scratch is all that is needed," Slade taunted.

"Needed for what?" Celina cried. "Mindy's mark was on

her neck."

Slade's smile was slow to come, and when it did finally arrive, it made Celina shiver. "Enjoy what's left of your life."

* * * * *

Celina thought about Slade's parting shot as she polished off a bottle of wine. The scratch on her arm burned. She'd poured rubbing alcohol over it to clean the wound, but nothing stopped the pain.

She picked up her phone and drunk dialed Mindy. It was her fault that Slade wasn't here. If she hadn't flirted shamelessly with all the men, none of this would've happened.

Mindy picked up, her voice sleep-filled. "Hello?"

"You think you're so s-special," Celina slurred. "But you're not."

"Celina?" Mindy asked. "Have you been drinking?"

"No, I'm drunk," she said. "Wolves are circling you and you're too clueless to know it."

"What?" Mindy asked. "Celina, you're not making any sense. You should go to bed. We'll talk in the morning, when you've sobered up."

Celina balked. "You-you-you don't see what's right in front of you. You're blind to the truth," she said. "Izzy knew. Probably why she left."

"I'm going to hang up now, before one of us says something that we'll regret," Mindy said.

"Too late!" Celina snapped. The empty wine bottle toppled onto its side. "You have already ruined everything for me."

Chapter Twenty

Mindy awoke blurry-eyed and confused the next morning. It had taken two hours to get back to sleep after she hung up with Celina. Her friend had said a lot of hurtful things, but Mindy knew it had been the alcohol talking.

What had gotten her friend so wound up was a mystery. A mystery Mindy planned to solve this morning.

She picked up the phone and punched in Celina's number. The phone rang five times, then her voicemail picked up. Odd, since Celina was an early riser. Was she screening her calls or too hung over to respond? It just didn't make sense.

Nothing about the last twenty-four hours made any sense. The outgoing message finished and was followed by a beep.

"Hey, Celina, it's Mindy." Words failed her. "We need to talk. I'll be over in an hour." Mindy hung up and wandered into the living room.

Nic was lying on the couch with an arm thrown over his eyes and his long legs propped up. His chest rose and fell evenly. He'd insisted on sleeping on the couch after Mindy told him that she had a perfectly good spare bed. Nic had smiled at her and said the only bed he wanted to sleep in was hers.

She tiptoed into the kitchen. Mindy had made it to the door when Nic said, "Morning beautiful."

Mindy stopped and glanced over her shoulder. His amazing eyes were fixed on her. Suddenly she wished she'd put on something nicer than her sweats.

"How'd you sleep?" she asked. No way had he been comfortable. Her couch had a lump in the middle of one of the cushions.

"Pretty good." He sat up and stretched.

"I'm going to make coffee," she said, watching the play of muscles beneath his shirt. "Want some?"

"That'd be great." He grinned. "But first I'm going to grab a shower."

Mindy nodded and slipped into the kitchen. Her fingers shook as she measured out the scoops and filled the tank. She pressed brew and walked back into the living room. She'd just finished feeding her gang when she heard whimpering outside.

The sound tugged at Mindy's heart. She threw the bolt on the front door and stepped out onto the porch. The hybrid was in the middle of her lawn, half-standing, half sitting. When he saw her, he dragged himself forward, his back legs limp beneath his big body.

"Oh no!" Mindy rushed off the porch and crouched down next to him. "What happened?" She scanned the canine from head to tail, but didn't immediately spot any blood. Had he been hit by a car again?

Mindy stood. She needed to get him into the car, get him to the clinic. "It's okay," she cooed, and stroked his head.

"Mindy, get away from him," Nic said.

She glanced toward the front door and saw Nic standing on the porch. He had a towel wrapped around his trim waist, his hair was slicked back, making it appear darker than it really was, and water dripped down his chest.

Normally a sight like that would disengage her brain, but

something about his tone frightened her. "It's okay," she said. "He isn't wild."

Nic stepped down from the porch. "You're in mortal danger. Move away from him slowly."

She frowned. What did he mean by that? "I know he's big, but he's really a teddy bear. Trust me," she said.

* * * * *

Nic was breathing hard. Not from exertion, but from sheer terror. Mindy didn't understand. He needed her to move away from the Darkling before it killed her. If it drew blood in any way, she was dead.

"Mindy, I need you to come to me." He took another step forward. "I know I'm asking a lot, but I need you to trust me one more time. That isn't what you think it is."

She stroked the massive creature's head. "It's a hybrid. A wolf dog," she said.

Nic moved closer. The first wave of magic licked his skin. He closed his eyes and let it roll over him. "No, honey, it's not. It's a Darkling."

"I don't know what that is." Mindy stared at him in confusion. "Nic, you're scaring me."

Before he could respond, the second wave of power struck. This time it hit like a tsunami, weakening his legs, driving him to his knees. Nic's head dropped back. "Oh goddess, no!" he cried as fur rippled over his arms and down his legs. The towel fell as his big body contorted. His wails quickly turned to howls.

* * * * *

Mindy stared in horror, not truly understanding what she was witnessing. No sign of Nic remained after the transformation. In his place stood a brindle-furred beast with a long snout, sharp claws, and massive teeth.

"Nic?"

The creature's head dropped and it stalked forward, baring its fangs and growling. Mindy knew this was it. She was about to be ripped to shreds. All the stories Izzy told her through the years came rushing back.

Izzy is right. There are monsters in the world.

The beast rushed her. Mindy closed her eyes. He hit her legs hard, sending her flying off to the side. Mindy landed in the grass and immediately rolled to her feet as the two animals came together in a clash of claws and teeth.

They tore at each other, ripping chunks of fur and flesh off. Blood covered their sides as they broke apart and attacked again and again. Mindy couldn't seem to tear her gaze away from the horrific sight.

She'd seen dogs fight, but their aggression had been nothing like this. These two creatures were trying to kill each other. Nic might actually die. Mindy's heart exploded in her chest. The thought of him dying left her bereft, left her more frightened than she'd been when she'd discovered Marco's body at the base of her steps.

* * * * *

Nic had to block Mindy's terrified expression out of his mind. One look at her face had told him that he'd lost her, but there was nothing he could do about that now. His heart had nearly stopped beating when he saw her so close to the Darkling.

All the stories about their abilities were true. The Darkling's magic had called to his wolf and demanded that it reveal itself.

Now Nic was in a fight for his life—for both their lives. He could feel his body weakening, but didn't dare let up.

The Darkling's magic wrapped around him, siphoning his power drop by drop. Soon he wouldn't have the strength to continue to fight.

He had to end this. Trouble was, they were evenly matched.

Blood dripped into his eyes and matted his fur. Nic stumbled, but somehow managed to stay on his feet. The Darkling struck again, tearing a furrow down his side. The magic burned like acid, eating at his skin.

Nic whimpered at Mindy. Tears streamed down her face. *Run!* he tried to shout, but all that came out was a fierce bark.

He swayed. He wouldn't last much longer. There was a reason why Darklings were the bogeymen of the Kin. Just stay awake long enough to get her to safety. His mate's safety was the only thing that mattered to him.

Nic latched on to the Darkling's leg and shook his head, trying to tear it off. The move didn't work, but it did leave his neck open for a counterattack.

* * * * *

Fear made Mindy finally move. Nic was hurt. Blood was everywhere. With the hybrid gripping his throat, he wouldn't last much longer. She had to do something. She scanned the yard for a weapon. There was nothing.

Mindy ran to the side of the house. The only thing there was a hose. She snatched it up and checked to make sure her power-washer nozzle was screwed on tight. As weapons went, it wasn't much.

She turned the water on and ran back to the front yard. Nic was lying on his side, but he hadn't completely given up. Mindy pointed the nozzle at the animals and squeezed the trigger.

Water blasted the hybrid in the face, shocking him enough to release Nic. He turned toward her and snarled. Mindy sprayed him again.

"Bad doggies!" The words brought out a giggle that threatened to release the hysteria Mindy held inside.

The hybrid snorted and shook his head, sending crimson droplets in every direction. Nic was trying to struggle to his feet, but couldn't seem to manage. The hybrid stalked Mindy. Nic threw his head back and howled. The sound was different, but she didn't have time to analyze the "hows" or the "whys."

"Stay back!" She held up the nozzle in front of her like it was a gun.

The beast hesitated, then kept coming.

"I'm warning you." She glanced over her shoulder to judge the distance to the door. Mindy didn't think she could make it to the house before he got her. "Don't move," she said, hoping he could understand her.

He kept coming.

A streak of bright orange ran past her legs. Hannibal's fur was raised, along with his tail. He yowled and spat at the hybrid, but it paid no attention to him.

That was until her cat launched himself onto the creature's back and clamped down on his ear. The hybrid snarled as Hannibal's claws dug into his fur, finding the tender skin beneath. He tried to shake the cat off, but the tabby held on tight.

The hybrid raised a claw to rip Hannibal away. Mindy blasted him in the face with the water before he could touch him. Water sprayed everywhere, including onto her cat. Hannibal leapt off the hybrid's back and ran into the house.

More howls filled the air. This time they weren't coming from Nic. The hybrid cocked its head to listen, then took off toward the woods.

When Mindy was sure that he was gone, she walked over to Nic. He was on his side, bleeding, and he didn't appear to be conscious. Mindy didn't want him in the house, but she couldn't bring herself to leave him out here.

She went into the house and got a beach towel, then laid it next to the beast. Mindy rolled "Nic" onto the towel and dragged him across the lawn. She was glad he was out cold, because there was no way to get him up the stairs without causing him more pain.

Mindy got him down the hall and into Tart's doggie cage. She was grateful that she'd decided to buy the largest one. If she hadn't, there was no way he would've fit. As soon as she had him inside, Mindy went into her bathroom to retrieve her first-aid kit.

Nic didn't stir as she cleaned his wounds and stitched him up. Mindy bandaged him quickly, then locked the cage. Blood covered her hands. Nic's blood. She even had a streak across her cheek.

She'd done everything she could think of to save him. For a second, she'd thought about taking him to the clinic, but Mindy quickly dismissed the idea. Nic wasn't an animal and he wasn't *human*.

Werewolf.

The insidious word whispered through her mind. Mindy's hands trembled. Werewolves weren't real. Monsters weren't real. This had to be a nightmare. Soon she'd wake up and Nic would be sleeping on the couch. Everything would go back to normal.

She stared at herself in the mirror. Nothing would be normal after today. Mindy couldn't go back to pretending that none of this was real. Nic was a monster. The kind of monster Izzy had warned her about.

He was also the man who'd saved her from Marco and Emmett. And the man who'd fixed her car. And the man who'd made love to her like she was the only woman on the planet who mattered to him. The question was, which one was the *real* Nic La Croix?

Mindy turned the water on in the shower as hot as she could stand it, then stripped out of her clothes and stepped under the spray. It hurt, but she didn't care. Mindy scrubbed and scrubbed until her skin glowed bright pink and there was no trace of blood swirling around her toes.

What was she going to do now?

She needed to call Celina, but she wasn't sure how much her friend knew. Nic had gone to a lot of trouble to keep his secret. Mindy couldn't betray his trust. He might have misled her, but he'd also saved her life. That counted for something.

CHAPTER TWENTY-ONE

Nic groaned and came to slowly. Every muscle in his body ached. He moved and felt a sharp pain in his side. He touched the spot and encountered gauze. What the hell happened to him?

He inhaled and caught Mindy's intoxicating aroma, then slowly opened his eyes. Bars came into view. Had he been arrested?

His hand slipped down, hitting bare skin. He was naked. That wasn't a good sign, if he was in jail. Nic blinked, trying to clear his vision and foggy head.

Something meowed.

Nic turned his head to find Mindy's one-eyed orange tabby, Hannibal, glaring at him. He scanned the bars again. They surrounded him. Not jail. A cage.

Fear enveloped him. Nic sat up quickly. His head banged against the top of the cage and he yelped. Hannibal sniffed at him, then turned tail and strolled silently out of the room. He looked around, but didn't recognize the bedroom. How had he gotten in here?

Mindy arrived in the doorway. A wary expression shadowed her soft features. "I thought I heard movement," she said. "Glad you're finally awake."

Nic shifted to sit up, but with his wide shoulders and large frame he couldn't move much. "What happened? How long have I been in here?" It was obvious that whatever occurred was bad—really bad, if he was locked inside a dog cage.

Mindy's eyes widened. "You don't remember?"

He shook his head and groaned again, clutching his temple. "No," he said. "How did I end up in here?"

She bit her lower lip. Despite his weakness and confusion, his body responded to the innocent act.

"I put you in there," she murmured. "Four hours ago."

The effect of her words was like being doused with cold water. Everything in him deflated. Four hours? A lot could happen in that time period.

"Why would you..." Memories of a garden hose and a fight came rushing back. "Mindy, I'm not sure what you think you saw—"

"Save your breath, Nic," she said. "I *know* what I saw."

The conviction in her voice cleared the last of the cobwebs out of his head. He had to do damage control. "I can explain," he said.

"No need," Mindy replied.

Nic's heart sank. "Let me out of here and I'll get my clothes and leave."

"Is it safe?" Her voice cracked. "I mean are you going to go all furry again?"

"You were never in any danger from me," he said softly. "I was serious when I said I'd protect you with my life."

Mindy unlocked the cage and opened the door. The second it swung wide, she stepped back out of reach.

Nic crawled and scooted, feeling every kink in his body start to relax. He was still in pain, but at least he was no longer cramping. He stood and stretched, unconcerned by his nudity. Nic inhaled, expecting to smell Mindy's fear, but there was none. Only quiet resolve. The kind of resolve one got when they had decided to cut their losses.

He had lost her. The one woman who meant everything to him. "Why didn't you run when you had the chance?" he asked.

Mindy scowled at him. "I couldn't."

"Why?" Nic needed to know. Her answer was vitally important to him.

"You needed my help," she said, and turned away.

He grabbed her hand to keep her from going. "You saw what I became. What made you think I needed your help?"

Mindy shrugged, but didn't try to pull away when he ran his thumb across her knuckles.

That is a good sign, isn't it?

"You were bleeding, Nic," she said. "Bad. It took me thirty minutes to get you stitched. You bled through two of the bandages."

He sensed her fear for the first time. Nic tasted it on the air, drew it into his lungs. Mindy hadn't been scared of him, at least after she got over the initial shock. She'd been scared *for* him. Hope glimmered inside him.

"I heal quickly," he said.

Their eyes met and clashed.

"He was going to kill you," she said softly. "I couldn't let that happen." Her confession ripped a hole in his gut.

"Neither could I," he whispered, willing her to understand.

Tears shimmered in Mindy's eyes. "Just because I saved you doesn't mean that I'm okay with any of this," she said. "I don't see how this can work. How we can work. We're two different species."

"It can and it will, if you just give us a chance," he said, believing it for the first time. Nic yanked Mindy into his arms and kissed her gently, tenderly. Her body softened, while his grew rigid.

Mindy pushed out of the embrace. "You're hurt," she said breathlessly.

Nic glanced down at the hard evidence of his desire. "Not that part of me."

"Nic, I can't do this right now," Mindy said. "I need time to process what's happened. To make sense of it all. It's not every day you find out that mon—"

"Monsters are real," he finished for her.

Mindy wasn't able to face him. "You understand. Don't you?"

He did, which was why it hurt so much. "I'll get my things," he said. Nic had to report to Aidan now that he had confirmation of the Darkling. "You take as much time as you need." He prayed she wouldn't take long, wouldn't take forever.

* * * * *

Watching him go was one of the hardest things Mindy had ever had to do. Nic looked so lost, so confused. Twice she found herself opening her mouth to call out and ask him to come back. But she didn't. She couldn't. Not until she sorted through her feelings.

As Nic drove away, Mindy picked up the phone and dialed Celina's number. She had a feeling this was what her friend had been trying to tell her last night when she called. If she knew Nic was different, why hadn't she just said so?

The phone rang and rang. Once more, the voicemail answered. "Celina, it's me again. I'm coming over."

The truth didn't hit Mindy until she was almost to Celina's apartment. Nic had said the hybrid was dangerous. Did he mean it was like him?

She'd never seen it look like anything but a canine. Celina had taken the hybrid home with her. Had she known what it was all along? Or had Celina been clueless like her?

Fear had her accelerating. Mindy couldn't believe that Celina would keep something so important from her. What did that say about their friendship?

The parking lot was full of emergency vehicles when Mindy arrived at the run-down apartment complex. *It could be anything*, she told herself, but she knew that it wasn't. She threw her car into park and jumped out as Celina came down the stairs on a gurney.

Mindy rushed forward, only to be cut off by the police. "That's my friend," she said. "You have to let me through."

"We can't," the officer said. "The medics think she's contagious."

"With what?" she demanded.

"Miss, I need you to take a step back," he said.

"Can you at least tell me where they're taking her?" she asked.

"Forest Mercy General," the officer said.

As the stretcher rolled by, Mindy got a close look at Celina's face. It was pale and streaked with makeup. Red blisters ringed her mouth and pink foam bubbled from her lips. Celina's body thrashed. If she hadn't been strapped in, she would've fallen off.

"Werewolves are everywhere!" she shouted. "Can't you see them? You're one of them," she blurted at the paramedic. "You don't love me! You just want to bite and scratch me!" Celina struggled some more. "I'm not a chew toy! Ahwoo! Ahwoo!" Her words faded into unintelligible growls and screams.

Mindy's stomach clenched. What happened to Celina? Was she going to be all right? Had the hybrid done that to her? How could it possibly have done this to Celina, when it had been around *her* house?

"Does she have rabies?" she asked the paramedic before he shut the ambulance door.

"We don't know," he said. "Do you know her?"

"Yes," she said. "She's a close friend and I work with her."

"Do you know if she's been bitten or scratched by anything in the past few days?" he asked.

Mindy opened her mouth, but no words would come out. She wanted to help Celina, but she couldn't tell them the truth. They'd think she was insane.

"I don't know," she answered honestly, but she knew someone who might. "We work at the animal clinic, so it's possible."

Mindy's hand covered the mark on her neck and her head swam, as the reality of what Nic was came crashing down upon her.

The officer reached for her. "Are you okay?" he asked.

"I'm-I'm..." She clutched her chest and nausea swamped her. Mindy ran to the back of her car and threw up. Was the same thing that was happening to Celina going to happen to her, too?

"Miss, do you need me to call another ambulance?"

Mindy hadn't heard the officer approach. She wiped her mouth with the back of her sleeve, then righted herself with the help of her car. "No, I'm okay now," she lied.

She climbed into her car and started the engine. Mindy pulled around the corner out of sight and stopped. She hugged herself as the ambulance drove by, sirens screeching. She needed to get to the hospital to find out what happened to Celina. Only then would she be able to say for certain that she'd be okay.

Chapter Twenty-Two

By the time Mindy reached the hospital and parked, she'd calmed down enough to think. She'd wanted time to process everything before she called Nic, but Celina's grave condition changed everything. She pulled her cell phone out of her purse and dialed Nic's number.

He answered on the first ring. "Mindy, now's not a good time." He sounded stressed.

"An ambulance took Celina away as I got to her apartment. She was foaming at the mouth and babbling about werewolves. They think she's contagious." She sniffled. "I thought you should know."

"Where are you?" he asked.

"I'm outside of Forest Mercy General," she said. "I'm going in now to see how she's doing."

"I'll get there as soon as I can." Nic disconnected the call.

* * * * *

"We have a problem," Nic said to Aidan.

"I heard," Aidan said. "Go! We'll deal with the Darkling later."

"Thanks." Nic bolted for the door.

"Nic!" Aidan's stern voice stopped him in his tracks.

He turned back to look at his Alpha.

"She'll be dead within two weeks," Aidan said.

His heart dropped. How could he tell Mindy that her friend was dying? If she connected the illness to the Darkling, she'd never let him near her again.

"You're certain that nothing can be done?" Nic asked. "Human medicine has advanced over the years."

Aidan's amber eyes softened. "Only Sighted-Ones can survive being marked by a Darkling," he said. "As you learned today, their magic is powerful—and lethal."

"Do you think there's a chance she's a Sighted-One?" Nic asked.

Aidan shook his head. "He wouldn't have left her if she was."

"What about Mindy?" Nic asked. "She's not a Sighted-One, yet the Darkling continued to pursue her. He showed up at her home repeatedly." He still couldn't believe that Darklings were real or how close to death Mindy had come. It left Nic shaken to his core.

Aidan shrugged and sat back in his seat. "Hard to say what its motives are. Darklings are nothing if not unpredictable. Perhaps it was drawn to her kindness or to something in her house?"

Blood drained from Nic's face. "Isabel," he said.

Aidan's brow furrowed. "Who's Isabel?"

"Mindy's sister," Nic said. "She told me that Izzy was Sighted. I didn't press her for more information at the time because it wasn't important."

Aidan came to his feet. "Where is Isabel now?"

"New Orleans," Nic said. "She should be safe, since the Darkling is here."

"We haven't been able to locate it," Aidan said. "It can hide its scent if it chooses to. We need a special tool to track it. One that can detect its magic. Until we have that in hand, we won't know where it is for sure."

"I doubt it would leave Mindy. It's stayed by her this whole time," Nic said. His wolf grumbled and struggled to break free. Even with the wounds inflicted upon it, it was ready to take the Darkling on again.

"I hope you're right," Aidan said. "For our sake and for Isabel's."

* * * * *

Nic arrived at the hospital. The second Mindy saw him, she rushed into his arms. He didn't care that a temporary need for solace was what drove her to him. Nic would accept any excuse to hold her.

"What did the doctors say?" he asked.

Tears spilled down her cheeks. "They won't let me see her. There's a big hazard sign outside her door." She pointed down the hall to the closed doors at the end.

"The hybrid had to have done this to her," Nic said.

Mindy shook her head. "I don't think so," she said. "I got the impression that Celina hadn't seen the hybrid in a while."

A doctor came out of the restricted hallway. Mindy rushed him. "How is Celina doing? Does she have rabies? Was she bitten?"

Rabies was lethal if it wasn't treated in time. Nic wanted to tell Mindy that Celina didn't have rabies, but he didn't think she'd listen to reason right now.

The doctor's pale brow lowered. "There's no sign of a bite, but we have located a scratch that appears to be infected."

"With rabies?" Mindy asked.

"No," the doctor said. "We haven't been able to identify the pathogen." His expression turned grave. "We're doing everything we can for her. Is there anything you can tell us? Anything at all that might help us narrow down the possibilities?"

Mindy stared at Nic accusingly and her lip quivered. "Sorry, I wish I could help," she said. "Is she going to make it?"

"It's too early to tell," the doctor said noncommittally. "But you may want to contact her family."

"She doesn't have any." Mindy turned to Nic after the doctor walked away. "I don't understand. If it's not rabies, then how could a scratch make Celina so sick?" She took a step back and touched the mark on her neck. "I have more than a scratch. You need to tell me if you think I'm going to get sick, too."

How could she think he'd be so careless with her life? "You're not going to get sick. Not from me."

Myriad emotions played across her face. In the end, Mindy didn't look entirely convinced that he was telling the truth. "You called the hybrid a Darkling. If it's something different than what you are, surely your people have cures or treatments against it."

"We are not the same species, though we do resemble one another," Nic said softly. "I would give anything to be able to help your friend, but there is nothing we can do for her."

* * * * *

Blood roared in Mindy's ears. What did Nic mean by that? "Are you saying Celina's going to die?"

Shadows filled his blue eyes and his face pinched with pain. "I'm sorry," he said. "Nothing can be done now."

Mindy shook her head. "I don't accept that. You may have given up on Celina, but I haven't." She grabbed her purse and walked down the sterile hall toward the elevators.

"Where are you going?" Nic asked. His long legs ate up the distance between them.

"I'm going to find the hybrid," she said. "If your people can't help her, then maybe he can."

Nic grabbed her arm and swung her around. "Are you insane? Did you see what that thing did to your friend?"

Mindy glared at his hand until he released her. "Yes," she said. "That's why I'm going."

"We haven't been able to find it," Nic said.

She pressed the button to call the elevator. "Maybe you've been looking in the wrong place."

The doors open and she stepped inside. Nic followed.

"Where do you plan to look?" he asked.

"I'm going to start with Celina's apartment," she said.

* * * * *

Celina's apartment had been sealed by the police. Mindy stared at the crime-scene tape.

"What now?" Nic asked.

She reached into her purse and pulled out a scalpel. "Now we go inside," Mindy said.

"That's illegal," he said.

Mindy glared at him. "I'm aware of that. You don't have to come in."

"You don't know what you're looking for," he said.

"Neither do you," she said.

She cut through the tape and opened the door. The scent of Darkling smacked Nic in the face and made his hackles rise.

"It was here," he said.

"Of course it was." Mindy stepped into the apartment. "Celina brought him home with her, before turning him over to the sanctuary."

"She lied about that," Nic said, glancing around the small space.

"I know," Mindy said quietly. "He's been coming around my house for a few days now."

"The scent is really strong," Nic said. "Like he was here recently. I'd say within the last few hours."

Mindy shook her head as she opened a cupboard. "That's impossible. I was here a few hours ago and so were the police. There was no one around. Not even her boyfriend, Slade."

"Slade?" Nic slowly turned to look at her. "Have you seen him?"

"No," Mindy said. "I expected him to show up at the hospital, but it's possible I missed him."

"What does he look like?" Nic asked.

"Dark hair, amber eyes, good-looking." She shrugged. "Celina's usual type." Mindy's eyes widened. "Do you think that Slade did this to her? Are he and the hybrid the same creature?"

"I can't say for certain," Nic said. "But it stands to reason."

Mindy clutched her stomach. "That makes no sense. Celina loved Slade. He knew that. She put up with all his crap."

"Darklings cannot feel *human* emotions," he said.

Mindy stiffened. "Are you telling me that you feel nothing for me? That all that tenderness was just an act?"

Nic rushed to her side. "No!" he barked. "I'm *not* a Darkling."

"I know you keep saying that," she said. "But I don't understand the difference."

Nic brushed her cheek. "The difference is that I love you."

Her eyes grew to the size of saucers and her breath seemed to stop. "I can't deal with that right now."

He did his best to hide the pain her rejection brought. "Let's check the bedroom, but I think he's gone."

They searched Celina's bedroom, but couldn't find any male clothes.

"Where do you think he went?" Mindy asked.

"Hopefully far, far away from this place," Nic said, praying it was true.

CHAPTER TWENTY-THREE

Jenna walked into Aidan's office. He put the phone down when he saw her. His gaze warmed as it settled on her swollen stomach.

"Did you know that Nic took a mate?" she asked.

Aidan slowly nodded.

"Were you going to tell me?" she asked.

Jenna made it sound like a simple question, but Aidan knew it was anything but. His bondmate never went the simple route.

"I only just learned about the situation when the police arrived," Aidan said. "There hasn't been time to have a true discussion."

Her long strawberry-blonde hair bounced as she lowered herself into the chair. "Don't you think we should've met her first?" Jenna paused. "Nic's tough on the outside, but he's tender-hearted on the inside. I don't want him to get hurt."

Aidan melted inside. "I understand, but as you recall, I didn't have much to do with the decision of taking you as my bondmate," he said. "My wolf was determined to claim you with or without my permission."

Her brow arched. "Are you saying that you didn't want

me?"

His lips canted and his eyes narrowed. "The first time I laid eyes on those legs of yours, I wanted to bend you over my desk and wrap my fist around your long hair."

Aidan looked at her stomach pointedly. "Obviously that's something my wolf and I could agree on."

Jenna giggled. "You're incorrigible."

"Yes." He grinned. "But you love me anyway."

She heaved herself out of the chair. "I have to go. The baby is hungry again."

She'd been using that excuse every time she needed to raid the kitchen. Aidan had ordered the chef to prepare a shelf just for her.

"You coming?" She waddled toward the door.

"I'll be there in a minute," Aidan said. "I have to make a phone call first."

"Don't take too long," Jenna said. "Or there won't be anything left."

"I won't." Aidan waited for her to shut the door, then lifted the receiver. He hit speed dial and waited for the Lycanian High Council to answer.

"What do you need, Aidan?" Tristan asked, forgoing pleasantries.

"A Darkling has entered our realm. It has killed one of my pups and has infected a human woman," Aidan said. "She's been hospitalized."

Silence met his statement.

"Tristan?" Aidan asked.

"Do you know where it is now?" Tristan asked.

Aidan could hear drawers opening and closing, then the sound of a zipper. "Not for certain. It was in the woods outside of Telegraph Road, but we haven't been able to find it. I have my best trackers scouring the area. It's possible the Darkling has moved on," he said.

"Where?" Tristan asked.

Aidan thought about what Nic had told him. "Perhaps

New Orleans."

"But you are not certain," Tristan said.

"No," Aidan replied. "It's able to mask its scent."

"Why would it go to that city and not another?" Tristan asked.

"There is a Sighted-One down there," Aidan said. "Isabel's related to the mate of one of my wolves."

There was more shuffling and a grunt. "Is the human woman in the hospital a Sighted-One?" Tristan asked.

"No," Aidan said softly.

"Then she will die," Tristan said matter-of-factly.

"I'm aware of that," Aidan said, gritting his teeth.

Tristan didn't care for humans and never hid his disdain for them. He'd shown up on Aidan's doorstep after he'd bondmated Jenna to ensure that the bond was real and that he'd bred true. Like other Elders, Tristan didn't like that two of the Alphas had chosen humans for mates. As if they'd had a choice in the matter. Aidan snorted.

"Stop gritting your teeth. I will begin the hunt now," Tristan said. "You may not sense me when I enter your territory."

Aidan could hear the smile in Tristan's voice. "I'll know you're here," he said. "Use caution with this one. The Darkling took down one of my biggest wolves. He's powerful."

Tristan laughed, the sound cold enough to freeze water. "So am I."

"Be sure to bring *Selene*," Aidan said.

"I never go anywhere without my sword. I'll use the lodestone to track him," Tristan said. "You'll know when it's done." He hung up.

Aidan dialed another number. This time the call went to his new assistant, Carson. "I want you to call all the wolves back to the estate. No one lives off property until the Darkling is found."

* * * * *

Four hours later, Tristan lingered in the woods outside of a small house off Telegraph Road. The scent of the Darkling was fading quickly, but he'd definitely been here. In this very spot.

Tristan ran his gloved hand over the ash stain, then studied the house again. It was small, well kept, with white walls and green window frames. He waited for the woman to leave her house, then broke inside.

The scent was nearly overpowering. A dog and cat rushed him, but one growl sent them scurrying away. Tristan followed the aroma down the hall. It led straight out the back door. He was about to leave when another scent caught his attention. This one lighter, almost citrusy in nature.

He stopped outside the door where the scent seemed the strongest, and inhaled. Tristan's head swam. He clutched the doorknob and twisted. The door creaked open and a comfortable bedroom came into view.

Tristan stepped inside and shut the door behind him. The citrusy scent filled the room. It was followed by a snap of magic. A Sighted-One had been here.

He scanned the area and saw a dresser shoved against the wall in the corner. There were framed photographs sitting on top of it.

He walked over and picked one up. There were two fair-haired girls smiling back at him. One had shoulder-length hair and looked a lot like the woman who'd driven off.

The other had a wild mane that didn't want to be tamed by the barrettes in her hair. Their arms were wrapped around each other, but the one on the left seemed distracted. Haunted.

"Isabel." He tasted her name on his tongue. The sound was as sharp and tangy as her scent.

Tristan ran his finger over the photo and smiled to himself. If he were a Darkling, he knew whom he'd pursue.

CHAPTER TWENTY-FOUR

It had been a month since Celina's funeral. The doctors still had no idea what had killed her, so they'd burned her clothes and suggested cremation. Since that was what Celina had wanted, Mindy had complied.

She hadn't seen Nic since the funeral. Mindy had told him that she needed time to grieve, time to digest, time to decide what she was going to do next. She still hadn't gotten over the fact that the hybrid had killed Marco and Celina because of her.

Guilt weighed heavily upon her shoulders, though she was aware that there'd been nothing she could've done to stop him.

Nic stayed away, but Mindy thought she'd caught glimpses of him in his wolf form, patrolling the edge of the woods. Occasionally, there'd been a single flower left on her steps. When that happened, she was reminded how much she missed him.

She had no idea how or if a relationship between them would work, but Mindy would regret never giving it a try.

The phone rang and she flinched, debating whether to let voicemail get it. It continued to ring. Mindy sighed and walked into the other room.

"Hello?" she asked.

"Mindy?" Izzy replied.

"Where have you been?" Mindy asked. "I've been trying to reach you for over a month. I thought something had happened to you. I was planning to fly down to Louisiana to find you."

"I'm sorry," Izzy said. "It's been kind of crazy around here."

"Celina's dead, Izzy." Mindy choked up.

There was a pause on the line, then Izzy said, "I know."

"If you knew, then why didn't you call?" Mindy asked.

"I couldn't," Izzy said.

Mindy opened her mouth to rip into her sister, but stopped short before she said something she'd regret. "I'm sorry."

"Sorry for what?" Izzy asked.

"Sorry that I didn't believe you," Mindy said. For the first time in her life, she truly understood her sister. "How were you able to live with the knowledge that there's more in this world than what meets the eye?" she asked. "I'm struggling, Izzy. Really struggling."

"I wish I could hug you," Izzy said. "It took a while to get past thinking I was crazy. Once I did, it took even more time to understand that the monsters weren't *all* evil. They're a lot like humans in that respect, but they do tend to be more loyal. Not that I hang around any of them. It's better if they believe I can't see them."

"How are you doing?" Mindy asked. "Do you need money?"

"I'm fine," Izzy said, but her voice cracked when she said it.

"Izzy, do you need me to come down there?" Mindy asked. "I can be on the first flight out tomorrow morning."

"No, I can handle what's going on. Remember, I've been doing this my whole life," Izzy said. "Besides, you're safer there."

A tear streaked down Mindy's cheek. "You were right about evil being here, but are you certain it's gone?"

"Yes, I am," Izzy said without hesitation.

"Then why don't I feel safe?" Mindy asked.

"It'll take time to adjust to your new reality," Izzy said. "I'm sorry I brought darkness to our door. I'm sure you've figured it out by now, but in case you haven't, you should know that it was after me."

Mindy had figured that out over the past few weeks. It had been the only thing that had made sense. "There's no need to be sorry," she said. "We handled it."

"We?" Izzy asked.

"I met someone." Mindy paused as she searched for the right words. "Well, *something*. We had a good thing going before I found out what he was, before the Darkling killed Marco, before Celina died, and everything fell apart."

Izzy sighed. "The world is complicated," she said. "We don't always get what we want, but sometimes we get what we need."

Mindy snorted. "You did *not* just quasi-quote a song."

Izzy laughed. "Maybe, but seriously, I have to lay low for a while. I may be out of touch."

"I'm coming down to get you," Mindy said. She wasn't about to let the Darkling or anything else get her sister. She'd already lost a friend and the man she was falling in love with.

"No!" Izzy shouted. "It's better if you stay where you are. He'll protect you."

"You haven't met him," Mindy said.

"I don't need to," Izzy replied.

"What's going on, Isabel?" Mindy asked.

"I'm not sure," Izzy said. "I think I'm being followed."

"By the Darkling?"

"I'm not sure," Izzy said.

"You need to call the police! Call them this instant!"

Mindy demanded. "I'll phone Nic, he'll know what to do."

"Is that his name?" Izzy asked.

People laughed in the background.

"Yes," Mindy said.

"Nice name," Izzy said.

The sound grew louder. "Izzy, where are you?"

"I'm in a bar, but I have to go. It's getting crowded. Stay safe. I'll be in touch when I can. And remember, he *will* protect you. Celina's spirit told me so." She hung up.

It was as close to a blessing as she'd ever get from her sister and from her dead friend.

Mindy's first reaction was to ignore Izzy's request to stay away and go to her aid, but she had no idea where her sister was staying or if she'd be there by the time she got to New Orleans. Was she being followed? If so, by whom? She prayed it wasn't the Darkling.

She plugged the phone into the charger and walked down the hall to the backdoor. Mindy opened it and stepped outside, then sat on the stairs. Darkness closed in around her. Had she ever felt this alone? Mindy couldn't recall.

In the distance, a lone wolf howled. The mournful sound echoed through the night and was answered by one much closer. Mindy stepped off the porch and scanned the tree line.

At first, she didn't see any movement, but as she continued to watch, a dark figure appeared out of the woods.

For a heartbeat, she thought it was the hybrid, then the animal came into focus. "Nic?"

Bones popped, muscles reshaped and fur faded, until the wolf was gone and Nic crouched in its place. He slowly stood, tall, trembling and fully erect. He didn't have a stich of clothing on as he hovered near the trees, and seemed completely at ease with his current state.

"I've missed you," Nic said.

"I've missed you too."

"Can we start over?" he asked.

She'd asked him the same question after their first night together. He'd said yes without hesitation. Could she?

Mindy turned and climbed the stairs. She stopped at the top of the porch and looked back. "You coming?"

* * * * *

Nic could hardly believe his ears, but he didn't have to be asked twice. He covered the distance between them in record time and pulled Mindy into his arms. His lips found hers tentatively at first, then he allowed the passion to ignite inside of him until they were both swept away.

Epilogue

Two months later...

"Are you sure you want to go through with this?" Nic asked. "You don't have to do this right now. We could wait until you have received word from Izzy. I know you're worried about her. We all are."

It was sweet of him to offer, but Mindy had made up her mind. There was no telling when she'd hear from Isabel. Her sister had made good on her promise to drop out of sight. No one had seen any sign of her, not even the man who'd been sent to New Orleans to find her.

She was still alive. Mindy could feel it, but Izzy wouldn't be in touch until she was ready. Besides, she'd given Mindy her blessing the last time they spoke.

Celina's death had taught Mindy that you couldn't put off happiness. You might not make it to that future moment, which was why she found herself standing in the middle of the woods surrounded by Nic's people.

"Let's do this," she said. Mindy took a deep breath.

"I'm right here with you." Nic smiled and squeezed her hand, then faced the pack. "I would like to present my bondmate to the Moonlight Kin."

Howls rose, growing in volume until the sound deafened.

Mindy's knees quivered as she stepped forward. *Don't throw up. Don't fall. Don't throw up. Don't fall.* The howls stopped instantly. Even the air seemed to still, waiting for what would happen next.

"You can do this," Nic murmured. "It's just like we practiced." A long claw slid out from the tip of his finger. When it surpassed four inches, Nic sliced the side of his neck.

Mindy's first reaction was to want to press her hand to the wound to stave off the bleeding, but she didn't. Instead, she waited like they'd rehearsed.

Once the blood flowed steadily, Nic leaned down so she could reach him.

Mindy framed his face with her hands and gently pulled him toward her. Her stomach gurgled, but there was no going back now. She pressed her lips against the wound and sucked. The coppery flavor on her tongue seemed unnatural, but she kept going.

Nic's body tightened and his arms locked around her waist. "More," he ground out, and shuddered.

Mindy sucked harder. Blood poured down her throat. She swallowed convulsively. How much would she have to drink to complete the ritual? She didn't think she could stomach much more.

Nic stopped her with a tender touch. "That's enough." He stroked her hair.

Mindy drew back and wiped the blood off her mouth. It stained her hands and shirt.

"It is done!" Nic shouted, and grinned at the pack. His teeth seemed longer than usual and his blue eyes were glowing.

A huge black wolf stepped forward, shape-shifting as he did so. Aidan turned to face the rest of the pack. "Let us welcome our new member with a hunt."

The wolves howled joyously.

As Mindy listened to their baying, her limbs began to tingle. "What's happening?" she asked Nic.

"It has begun," he said. "You're strong. You can do this."

Heat swept through her body. Mindy cried out as her first bone snapped. The pain was excruciating and she dropped to her knees.

"It's only painful the first time," Nic said, brushing her arm.

More bones broke and pale fur rippled over her arms. Mindy screamed as the world dimmed around her, then suddenly sprang into sharp relief.

She looked around and everything glistened with a silvery-gray hue. It was night, but Mindy could see every detail as clear as day. A massive brindle wolf nudged her, then nipped at her haunches.

Mindy took off through the woods with the pack running along beside her. The wind whipped through her fur, bringing with it all the tantalizing secrets that the trees kept.

She yipped excitedly.

The brindle wolf nudged her again, this time away from the others. Mindy was reluctant to go, but there was no fighting him.

When they were alone in a meadow, the wolf brushed its mouth against hers, then sniffed and licked her hind end with renewed interest. Fire swept through Mindy's body again as muscle and bone reshaped, but this time the pain wasn't nearly as numbing.

Nude and trembling, Mindy looked down at Nic and brushed his head with her fingertips. "I'm not sure that I'm that kinky," she said.

He gave her a toothy smile and slowly shifted back into human form. "There will be plenty of time for that later, bondmate," he said mischievously.

Mindy couldn't wait.

MOONLIGHT KIN 4: TRISTAN
UNEDITED EXCERPT

Jazz and blues rang out through the Jackson Square courtyard as street musicians turned up the volume and charm to compete for tourist dollars. Tonight the jazzy band at the end of the square had a lone trumpet player and a violinist attempting to lure their crowd away.

Along with the musicians, tarot and palm readers had already set up their tables, staggering them just enough to give the pretense of privacy.

Isabel "Izzy" MacDougal did a quick head count. There were ten total. Her table would make eleven and that was just counting the ones in Jackson Square. Others would be set up along the side streets near Bourbon St., hoping to catch the stray drunk ready to part with their hard earned cash.

Izzy scanned the crowd as she unfolded her small card table and spread her purple shawl on top of it. She spotted her friend Everly Watts a few tables over. Everly was a short, dark-haired Goth who resembled an anemic vampire. Most nights she could be found at The Dungeon with all the other Goths and vampire wannabes in town. The pancake makeup disguised her sensitive nature and fierce intelligence, but nothing could hide her street smarts. Everly waved, then went back to reading the woman seated across from her.

Not even dusk yet and the French Quarter in New Orleans was already bursting at the seams with sunburned tourists and crafty pickpockets.

Isabel finished setting up and took a seat. She kept her expression open, which was hard to do when she was continuously bombarded by impressions from the growing crowd. Unlike some of the others situated around the square, Izzy had a true gift of Sight.

She snorted. Some gift.

Though her abilities had been the reason she and Everly had hit it off. Everly understood what Izzy was going through because she saw monsters, too.

Instead of growing up in a loving household like Isabel, Everly had been kicked out of her home when her "gifts" arrived. According to the petite Goth, she'd been living on her own ever since. She survived by taking on menial jobs and never staying in one place for too long.

Izzy shuffled her tarot cards and smiled at a passing group of women who appeared to be part of a conference if their nametags were to be believed.

"Would you like to know what your future holds, ladies?" she asked.

One of the women giggled, but the ash blonde stopped to chat. "Can you tell me if I'm going to meet someone soon?" she asked.

"Sure," Izzy said. "Take a seat."

The woman's hand clasped the back of the folding chair as she pulled it out to sit down.

"Lisa, you're not really going to waste your money on that crap, are you?" her friend asked.

The blonde looked back at Izzy. This time there was uncertainty in her green eyes. Before she could get up, Isabel flipped the first card over.

"He has dark hair," she said.

The woman scooted forward on her seat. "Really?"

"Yes," Izzy said. "And he's tall."

"Is his name Mike?" Lisa asked, peering into the cards in search of answers.

Izzy closed her eyes and concentrated. She saw the dark-haired man in her vision drop down to one knee in front of the blonde woman.

"I see him proposing," she said. "It's quite a ring."

Lisa squealed. "Oh my god! When?"

Izzy examined her vision. The leaves on the trees around the couple were orange and red, but no limbs were bare. "The fall," she said, opening her eyes. "He'll propose in the fall."

The woman whipped her head around to look at her friends. "Did you hear that? Mike is going to propose to me in the fall."

The skeptic among them simply shook her head in exasperation. "Mike's a jerk," she muttered.

Izzy turned her attention away from the cards and stared at the woman. Her aura was dark, nearly black in some places. Isabel looked deeper, trying to peer past the outer layer so she could see what was causing her pain.

A red-haired man appeared in her mind, then quickly faded into a tombstone with the name Thomas carved into its gray rigid face.

"I'm sorry about Thomas," Izzy said. "He really loved you."

The woman's face went from red to white, as the blood drained out of her cheeks. "How did you know about him?" she whispered.

Izzy simply shrugged. She couldn't begin to explain where her "gift" came from and certainly not to someone who wasn't ready to listen.

"Think she's still a fraud?" Lisa asked as she plucked

several bills out of her wallet and laid them on the table.

"Let's go," the skeptic said. "I need a drink."

Izzy watched them get swallowed by the crowd. More people approached her. She got ten more readings done before her head threatened to explode. This was what happened every night. She could only read for so long before her "gift" exerted too much pressure and her body gave out.

She was packing her things, when the first inkling of unease struck. Izzy casually scanned the crowd, but no one seemed overly interested in her. She finished gathering her fortune-telling tools and shoved them into her backpack.

Izzy folded her table and chairs, then took them over to Everly. "Can you keep these for me until tomorrow?" Izzy asked.

Everly's back stiffened and she frowned. "Sure," she said, scanning the faces around them.

"It's okay," Izzy said. She knew whatever was out there didn't know about Everly—at least not yet. "I'm going to head out. Catch you later."

Everly nodded, but she didn't relax.

Izzy hurried through the crowd, cutting along Pere Antoine's alley before hanging a left toward St. Peter Street. She glanced up and down the sidewalk, then ducked into Yo Mama's Bar and Grill.

The bearded doorman greeted her with a friendly smile. Izzy grinned back, then bounded up the stairs where her friend Heather was bartending.

A red light illuminated the small space. Two couches, a couple of long tables, dancing statues, and a small bar filled the room. Classic rock from an old jukebox blared out of speakers mounted in the ceiling. The place reminded her of a bordello, but it had *amazing* hamburgers.

Izzy's stomach growled. She wished she had time to order one, but she needed to use Heather's phone, then get back to her apartment on Dumaine Street.

Heather had just popped the cap off a long-neck, when

she spotted Izzy. She smiled, then without saying a word, she grabbed her cell phone and tossed it to her. Izzy caught it easily, mouthed the word "thanks", and quickly called her sister, Mindy.

She didn't want to alarm sister, but Izzy needed to let Mindy know that someone was following her and she might have to lay low for a while. It would hurt to be out of touch with her sister, but Izzy didn't have much choice. The darkness she'd sensed in Breakbend, Oregon was now here and getting closer. She'd felt its presence growing and it terrified her.

Izzy finished up her call and handed the phone back to Heather. "Thanks," she said.

"Anytime," Heather said. "Catch you later?"

She shook her head. "Not tonight. I have a headache." Izzy rubbed her temples for emphasis.

"Catch you next time," Heather said, then moved onto a waiting customer.

Isabel hurried down the stairs, but stopped before she stepped out onto the sidewalk. The doorman was watching her, but didn't say anything since this wasn't exactly anything new from her.

"It's all clear," he said.

"Thanks." Izzy slipped out the door and headed toward Bourbon. She'd just passed Royal Street, when the sensation of being watched returned.

Izzy glanced over her shoulder, but didn't see anyone. There was nothing out of the ordinary. Ordinary being a relative term in the French Quarter. There was nothing around that should alarm her, but Izzy knew he was there.

She *felt* him.

She wound her way through the heavy crowd, hoping to lose her pursuer on raucous Bourbon St. When she got the chance, Izzy turned down Dumaine Street. The crowd was thinning now. She could see the beginnings of Louis Armstrong Park in the distance. The trees swayed as the sun sank and darkness took over.

This was their time. The time when they were the most comfortable. The time when the real monsters came out.

Izzy hurried along the uneven sidewalks. She could still hear music coming from Bourbon Street. The jumble of sounds and collision of smells should've comforted her, but Izzy knew she was alone.

She tripped over a raised concrete slab. Her hands clasped the wrought iron fence that ran along the front of one of the old gentrified homes and kept her from falling. The metal felt good in her hand. It was cool. It was hard. It was real—as real as the heavy footsteps coming up fast behind her. Izzy pushed away from the fence and hurried on.

Her heart was pounding so hard she could barely hear herself think. Izzy turned to get a look at who was approaching and collided with a wall. It wasn't until she turned her head that she realized it wasn't a wall. It was a man's hard chest.

Strong hands grasped her arms whether to keep her from falling or prevent her from leaving she didn't know. Izzy looked up. Her gaze collided with a pair of mercury colored eyes and she shivered, despite his handsome face.

Her body went from hot to cold to hot again. Staring in his eyes was like staring into the face of the Arctic. His white blond hair and stern expression was as unforgiving as the harsh tundra.

As Izzy watched, the image of a white wolf appeared over his human features. She felt the blood drain from her cheeks. "Let me go," she said.

He didn't release her. Instead, the man's grip tightened. "You're being hunted," he said.

She knew that. Izzy had known that for days. The odd part was that he announced it like he wasn't the one hunting her.

The man was the biggest monster she'd ever seen. He seemed unnaturally large for a werewolf and that was saying something, since they tended to be massive.

"Let me go or I'm going to scream," Izzy said.

"This is the French Quarter," he said. "No one will notice." His sensual lips tilted into a smirk.

Izzy wanted to knock that smirk right off his face.

As if reading her mind, his smile vanished. "If you don't come with me, you're going to die."

Despite the ominous and rather clichéd warning, Isabel had no intention of going anywhere with him. He was one of them. She'd seen his true form. She would be safer locked in a cage with a half-starved polar bear. Everything about this man screamed that he was dangerous.

A trashcan lid banged at the end of the street. They both turned to see what had caused the noise. Izzy took his momentary distraction as a chance to get away. She twisted out of his hold and took off running.

ABOUT THE AUTHOR

Jordan Summers has thirty-one published books to her credit. She's a member of the Science Fiction and Fantasy Writers of America, The Horror Writer's Association, International Thriller Writers, and Novelist Inc.

Connect with her online:
Twitter.com/jordanwriter
www.facebook.com/authorjordansummers
www.JordanSummers.com
Join the Endless Summers Newsletter to find out about
upcoming releases and author signings.
Click here to join now!

OTHER BOOKS BY JORDAN SUMMERS

Dead World Prequel: Raphael
Dead World Prequel: Kane
Dead World 1: Red
Dead World 2: Scarlet

Moonlight Kin 1: A Wolf's Tale
Moonlight Kin 2: Aidan's Mate

Phantom Warriors 1: Bacchus
Phantom Warriors 2: Saber-tooth
Phantom Warriors 3: Talon
Phantom Warriors 4: Arctos
Phantom Warriors 5: Linx
Phantom Warriors 6: Riot
Phantom Warriors 7: The Dark King
Phantom Warriors Anthology Volume 1
Phantom Warriors Anthology Volume 2

The Dark King

Atlantean's Quest 1: The Arrival
Atlantean's Quest 2: Exodus
Atlantean's Quest 3: Redemption
Atlantean Heat 3.5
Atlantean's Quest 4: The Return
Atlantean's Quest 5: The Dark King
Atlantean's Quest Bundle Volume 1
Atlantean's Quest Bundle Volume 2

Tears of Amun
Heat of the Night
Gothic Passions
Rose's Rapture
Paris After Dark

Ghost Hunter: Solomon's Seals

Private Investigations
Mesmerized
Hot Shot
Ride Em' Cowboy
Off Limits

www.ingramcontent.com/pod-product-compliance
Lightning Source LLC
Chambersburg PA
CBHW070259120726
47910CB00007B/2307